The
TAKEOUT

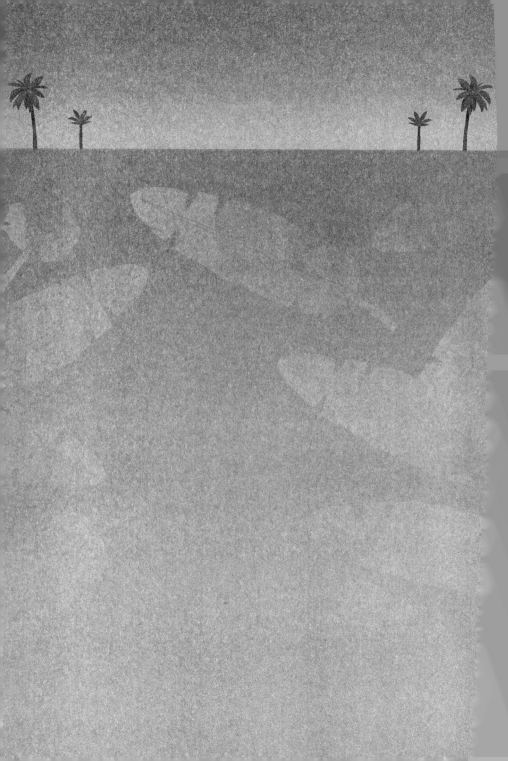

The
TAKEOUT

THE BANANA LEAF

TRACY BADUA

CLARION BOOKS

AN IMPRINT OF HARPERCOLLINSPUBLISHERS

Clarion Books is an imprint of HarperCollins Publishers.

The Takeout

Copyright © 2023 by Tracy Badua

All rights reserved. Printed in the United States of America.
No part of this book may be used or reproduced in any manner
whatsoever without written permission except in the case of
brief quotations embodied in critical articles and reviews. For
information address HarperCollins Children's Books, a division of
HarperCollins Publishers, 195 Broadway, New York, NY 10007.
www.harpercollinschildrens.com

Library of Congress Cataloging-in-Publication Data
Names: Badua, Tracy, author.
Title: The takeout / Tracy Badua.
Description: First edition. | New York : Clarion Books, [2023] |
    Audience:
Ages 8–12. | Audience: Grades 4–6. | Summary: Twelve-year-old Mila
    uses Filipino folk magic to take down the shady chef brothers who
    are threatening her family's food truck.
Identifiers: LCCN 2022031108 | ISBN 9780358671732 (hardcover)
Subjects: CYAC: Food trucks—Fiction. | Family-owned
    business enterprises—Fiction. | Magic—Fiction. | Filipino
    Americans—Fiction.
Classification: LCC PZ7.1.B275 Tak 2023 | DDC [Fic]—dc23
LC record available at https://lccn.loc.gov/2022031108

Typography by Celeste Knudsen and Laura Mock
23 24 25 26 27 LBC 5 4 3 2 1

First Edition

For Raja

1

PEOPLE SAY THAT HOME IS WHERE THE HEART is, but that's a lie. Home is where the *stomach* is. And my home is at the Banana Leaf, the best food truck in all of Coral Beach, California.

I switch off the blender. "Two turon lassis, coming right up!"

I wanted to call my signature drink the Mila Special. But Dad and Mr. Ram, Dad's best friend and business partner, thought "turon lassi" would remind customers more of the deep-fried Filipino snack and the refreshing yogurt drink from India. Even though my name sounds better, I let this one go. They technically own the food truck, after all. I've just lived, worked, and breathed in it since school let out for the summer.

I hand one plastic cup to Elle, a girl from my new school

who's been coming by twice a week for our lassis. I'd sat next to her when I first shuffled into the classroom in February, and even though she's friendly, I'm not sure she considers me a real friend yet. Oh, the joys of transferring mid–school year.

Elle's part of the Seashell Squad, a tight-knit group of four girls who have been friends almost since birth. Last year, other kids started referring to them as the Seashells because of their matching friendship bracelets, complete with shells dangling from them. They thought it was funny and embraced the name.

Next to Elle, another Seashell, Karina, balances on her retro blue bike and squints out at the beach. She didn't order anything.

"Thanks, Mila!" Elle says as she pulls out her phone. She snaps a picture of her drink against the background of our truck.

It's hard not to swell with pride. I helped come up with the truck design. The Banana Leaf is glossy red, with yellow trim around the windows. I painted the lush green banana trees all over the back: totally photo-worthy. I got so many likes and texts from my friends back in Los Angeles when we unveiled the truck on social media.

I almost hand the second turon lassi to another customer when I notice something off about her. She's an older teen with brown hair that looks like it hasn't been brushed and red all around her puffy eyes. She sniffles on the phone. "We were supposed to spend the summer together! And he breaks up with me?"

A broken heart? I remember my sister's latest breakup. I don't wish that kind of misery on anyone. Luckily, I may have a fix for this, at least a temporary one. *If* I can get it to work.

When the girl reaches for her drink, I hold it back slightly. I wave her closer so I can speak without the adults overhearing, then regret it when she sniffles right in my ear.

"I might have an all-natural potion that can help ease the heartache," I whisper, "but you have to keep it secret." I tilt my head toward Dad and Mr. Ram, the universal sign for "from these guys."

She lowers her phone. "All-natural? So it's not a drug or anything?"

I shake my head. "It's more like a tea: a bunch of herbs and roots steeped so they're super-concentrated. It's prepared by Filipino folk healers."

"Non-Western medicine? Cool. I saw an infographic about that. Sure, I'll try anything to get that jerk out of my mind."

I reach inside my enamel-pin-covered blue messenger bag and feel around for a small glass bottle, keeping an eye out to make sure Dad and Mr. Ram don't see. They wouldn't love the idea of magicking a customer's food. Dad didn't even approve of me adding double-washed (as opposed to triple-washed) cilantro to a customer's dish, for fear that someone might get a stomach bug and blame the truck.

But there's nothing to worry about with these blends. My sister, Catalina, has been studying Filipino folk healing for years, and she's re-created a few potions that help improve health and mood. They don't conjure up conditions and emotions that don't exist: they amplify what might already be there. So her immunity tincture might not cure me if I've already caught a cold, but if I need an extra boost of confidence for a school presentation I've prepared for, the right potion could give me the perfect leg up.

My few attempts at learning these potions have failed (and led to a couple of stomach bugs). But the ones I'm using now are my sister's. She made me practice the incantation out loud a hundred times, so I hope they'll work as well on the customer as they do on me.

I tug out the potion Catalina made for easing sadness. I thought she was coming with us when we moved to Coral Beach a couple of months ago, but she stayed in Los Angeles to take summer classes at the university. She made me what she calls Brightening Brew—she handwrites her own fun names on all the bottles because I can't pronounce Filipino ones right—to lighten my mood when I miss her too much.

I glance up. Dad is busy manning the deep fryer while Mr. Ram pokes at the register. Outside, Karina and Elle watch a dance video on Elle's phone, and the customer is still half sobbing through her phone conversation.

Carefully, with my back to everyone, I pour two drops into the customer's lassi and recall Catalina's written instruction for this Latin-ish incantation. I say Latin-*ish* because there's often a mix of Latin, Tagalog, Ilocano, and other Filipino languages in the incantations we must recite when using these potions. Folk healing in the Philippines took a lot of twists and turns throughout history thanks to influences from different faiths and parts of the world.

"*Claritas*," I whisper as I swirl the lassi around in its cup. I reapply the lid, pocket the potion, and hand the cup to her. "Here you go. You might catch an extra hint of cardamom in there," I say with a wink. Sometimes the taste of the more pungent potions can't be masked: I still can't drink Catalina's vinegary immunity potion without making a face.

"What do I owe you?" the girl asks.

I wave a dismissive hand. "No charge. But a good review of our truck—without mentioning the potion part—wouldn't hurt."

The girl nods and, back on the phone, takes a sip. "He said he needed space. What does that even mean?" Another sip, then her eyes flare with a flash of gold that tells me Catalina's potion is working. The wrinkle in her forehead relaxes.

"You know what? He can have all the space he needs. I'm"—she burps, sometimes a side effect of a potent potion—"happy all by myself. At least now I don't have to worry about someone eating my fries when he didn't order any." The girl mouths a "thank you" at me and walks off, her back a little straighter.

Karina lowers her phone and watches the customer practically march away. "Wow! I didn't think anything would cheer that girl up."

Elle pauses her sipping long enough to say, "Who wouldn't be in a good mood after this lassi? Honestly, Karina, you should try some." She offers her straw.

Karina dodges it. "No thanks. It just seems a little . . . exotic for me."

I force a smile and wipe a stray dot of lassi off my brown arm onto my old black Los Angeles tank top. Elle loves our truck's food, but I've learned from the times I've been invited to squeeze in at the Seashells' lunch table that Karina needs time to warm up to something that's not her usual. And that's why I'm not sure I should let them in on the secret about Catalina's magical herbal mixes.

Folks here in Coral Beach seem a little sugar-cookie-cutter, and when a bottle rolled out of my messenger bag

6

one day and Karina picked it up, the Seashells thought it was some new beauty product. Then their faces scrunched skeptically as Karina read aloud the mood-enhancing Brightening Brew instructions handwritten by my sister. They only relaxed when I spun it as a New Age alternative health practice, a little like how Elle's brother got really into essential oils during spring break. They don't know there's actual magic involved or that there's nothing "new" about it: my ancestors have been folk healers for ages. That may be too out-there for them. Karina's aunt is famous for petitioning the school to stop its yoga segment in PE because it was too "foreign."

When we first moved here, I was bright-eyed enough to hope that making friends wouldn't be too tough. But starting school in the middle of the year—and being the only chubby, short-black-haired, dark-brown-skinned Asian girl in a sea of beach mansion Barbies—sliced those hopes short. Everyone was already set into cliques; I couldn't even join the basketball team that late in the year.

To my surprise, Elle, Karina, and their similarly pink-lip-glossed Seashell Squad invited me to sit with them at lunch after they spied the food-themed pins on my bag. (The burrito with sunglasses never fails to spark conversation.)

We hit it off over our shared love of burritos, eye-catching accessories, and Cuisine Channel favorites. They're all nice and fun to hang out with, but they've lived in Coral Beach their whole lives. Their mothers belong to the same exclusive Coral Beach Belles Women's Club, a social group that raises funds for local causes like new computers at the library or cleaning bird poop off the town founder's statue.

I learned quickly that trying to be friends with the Seashell Squad means *being* like them—laughing at the same jokes, loving the same K-pop bands, watching the same shows—and not so much detailing my potion-brewing attempts. Hiding parts of myself so people will like me is still something I'm trying to get used to. It wasn't hard for me to find friends at my old school in LA, where there were plenty of fish in a wide, weird sea. So I wasn't prepared for suddenly feeling like the one kid with interests deemed unconventional by Coral Beach standards.

Grandma Flora always talks about the importance of fitting in. She moved to the United States in her thirties, with a thick accent that's since dulled. According to her, we should make an effort to be more like our US-born-and-raised neighbors (never mind that Catalina and I were actually born and raised here, too).

Today, I'm wearing palm-tree-shaped earrings like Elle's and the pink string friendship bracelet Karina made for me at the school's end-of-the-year field day. The bracelet doesn't have a seashell like the other girls', but it's a start. This is me trying to fit in.

"What are you two up to today?" I ask.

Elle takes another sip. Her curly light brown hair is pulled into a thick ponytail, and she's wearing a sunshine-yellow romper that matches her cell phone cover. "We've got ballet in a few minutes, but I had to stop for lassi on the way."

"Maybe we'll scope out the pier after. My mom said I get to pick where we're having dinner tonight." Karina flicks her shoulder-length blond hair behind her.

I wouldn't be able to mimic that move if I tried. First of all, I'm wearing a hair net. Second, I have the shortest hair of any girl in my grade.

"You look like a boy," Grandma says every time Dad and I come back from A Cut Above the Rest, Elle's sister's salon.

"And?" Dad and I reply.

Every. Time.

Grandma has a perfectly volumized straight black bob, and hardly goes anywhere—not even the grocery store— without gleaming pearl earrings and her signature red lipstick. Image is a huge deal to her, and somehow that extends to Dad and me, too.

In contrast to my food-stained short denim overalls,

Karina's in spotless white jeans and a sequin-dotted white crop top that Grandma would never let me out of the house in. Grandma holds a set idea of what "good American girls" dress like, and it's pretty much just a kid-size version of her blouses, slacks, calf-length dresses, and higher-end athleisure wear. Living with her—and slipping out of the house before she can demand an outfit change—has been a challenge.

"You and your dad are welcome to come to dinner," Karina adds.

Joy bubbles up in me: I'm invited to dinner! But before I can mention that my dad is probably stuck working his other job tonight, two big rigs rumble by, sending the ground beneath me vibrating. Tiny pebbles skitter around my shoes when a tour bus with dark, tinted windows follows.

My heart speeds up. This kind of traffic is new. The most exciting thing to happen during the four months we've been here was the ice cream parlor adding salt to its caramel. (They missed *that* trend by a decade, but Dad says it's rude for me to point it out, especially when he's trying to be best friends with everyone in the Coral Beach Chamber of Commerce.)

Dad's voice cuts through the noise. "How many lassis have we sold today?"

"That last sale makes thirty!"

He adjusts the sky-blue ball cap he keeps tugged down

over his stick-straight black hair. "That's got to be a record."

"What can I say? My signature drink is the most popular thing we've got."

Dad laughs. "I'd like to think my cooking draws a couple customers too."

"The lassi is so good, Mr. Pascual," Elle cuts in. "Have you considered selling a venti size?"

Mr. Ram points at a digital picture frame he's set up next to the iPad we use to take orders. The frame showcases the food photos our customers have posted and tagged on social media. His brown eyes, partially hidden by a curtain of long black eyelashes that I'm a little jealous of, scan the screen. "I'm siding with the girls on this one. The turon lassi with that crispy lumpia wrapper garnish? It's the most liked thing on our Instagram account. Look, we just got a five-star review!"

That review must have been from Breakup Girl.

"Most importantly," I add, "it's delicious." *And good for delivering helpful elixirs and tinctures*, but I leave that part out to keep the focus on the food and the magic my secret.

Like with Dad, my taste buds are in charge. We'll chase the yummiest bites, the most daring flavor combinations, the rarest and priciest ingredients. Mr. Ram, with his fancy business degree, keeps an eye on the more boring business side of the food truck. Mom went to the Philippines to help take care of my grandfather after his heart surgery, but when she was here, she helped add sparkle and laughter to the place. Still, with Dad as chef, Mr. Ram as the brains, and me as the muse and taste tester, we're a good team.

When Mr. Ram tears his eyes away from the screen, his mustache-topped lips dip into a frown. "New tenant's moving into the French spot?"

We all follow his gaze to the storefront that used to be Coral Beach's oldest and most expensive French restaurant. It was shuttered right before my family moved here. Over this past weekend, the boarded-up windows were replaced and the drab black and brown paint was switched out for vibrant pinks and greens.

I swing open the truck's back door, raising a hand to shield my eyes from the sun, and squint to see across the square. Sure enough, the pink doors of the former French restaurant are propped open. People are milling around inside, moving furniture and ripping plastic and paper off of things. What grabs my attention, though, is the camera crew setting up outside.

I cross my fingers. "Maybe it's a ghost-hunting reality show stop!"

Dad's voice has none of my excitement. "Or another restaurant?"

I hear the worry. The Banana Leaf's innovative Filipino and Indian fusion cuisine manages to garner us enough customers to stay shakily afloat. And that's after Dad and Mr. Ram both went part-time at their jobs, got a business loan, and put their savings at risk for something Grandma called "one of the worst ideas I've ever heard." With the recent downturn in tourism, a lot of other local businesses haven't been so lucky, something the vacant storefronts dotting Main Street remind us of every day.

Mr. Ram and Dad exchange a glance, and I can see the dollar signs wavering in the air between them.

"It could be anything," I offer.

"We do need another pet store," Elle says.

Karina's eyes brighten. "Or one of those fancy soap shops."

"Even if it's a restaurant, they've got nothing on us," I say. "Channel seven called us 'this year's food truck to watch.'"

Dad pats me on the shoulder, a gesture I think he means to be comforting but that only makes me more nervous. The last time he did it was when I got braces.

"You're right, Mila. I'm sure it's nothing to be worried about."

But the look Dad levels at Mr. Ram tells me it's something so worrisome that they won't talk about it with me around. I'm about to dig in more when the tour bus doors open. Out step two thin white men with fashionably gelled-back dark brown hair and pale, non-beach-town skin. They both wear black sunglasses, fitted khaki slacks, and button-down shirts (one in pink, one in green) with the sleeves rolled up to their elbows.

Karina and Elle practically squeal. My breath catches in my throat. I'd know those silhouettes anywhere. I've analyzed their every restaurant makeover, their every suggestion to tweak a menu or cut a bland, uninspired dish.

The Fab Foodie Brothers. Identical twins with a flair for helping failing restaurants spruce up their dining rooms, fire non–team players, and modernize menus.

I suddenly remember to breathe, and gasp so hard that I start coughing. Dad slaps me on the back. "Mila, what's wrong? Did you swallow a bug?"

Does he think I'm still a toddler? Twelve-year-olds don't swallow bugs! I can't believe he'd say that in front of my new friends.

"It's them!" I point across the square, certain my eyes have formed stars at the sight of the biggest celebrities on the Cuisine Channel. "Chip and Chaz Darlington!"

Dad's forehead scrunches. "So it *is* another restaurant. Like we need the competition."

"Huh," Mr. Ram says. He taps his foot, a counterpart to the gears turning in his head. "You know, Eddie, this could actually be good for us. Having a high-end celebrity restaurant in town could bring more customers. When they can't get a table there, we park the Banana Leaf right across the square or down the street, and voilà! Ready to serve."

Dad doesn't look convinced. I'm sure Mr. Ram will talk him down later, but for now, my legs tense, ready to dash over to explore. My heroes are here in the flesh, with only a quarter mile of grass, trees, and cement between us.

"We have to see what's going on," Karina says.

Elle's already got her phone out, no doubt texting the rest of the Seashell Squad.

"Can I go check it out too?" I ask Dad.

His face softens. He knows how much I love the Fab Foodie Brothers. He even deleted a *Star Wars* movie off Grandma's DVR so I'd have enough space for their Memorial Day special. It was a grand sacrifice on his end.

Chip and Chaz position themselves in front of the pink doors, their associates swirling around them. One pins microphones to their collars, the other brushes powder across their narrow noses. One simply stands three feet away, holding a vitamin-enhanced water in each hand.

I don't know what they're about to announce, but I know

I don't want to miss it. An inside scoop on the next season of *Fab Foodie Brothers*? Catalina and my LA friends would keel over in jealousy.

Dad sighs, his eyes clouding. "Go ahead."

I leap out of the back of the Banana Leaf. My friends bike away and I follow, leaving the scents of gasoline and hot cooking oil behind.

2

BY THE TIME I GET TO THE OLD FRENCH SPOT, a crowd has gathered. The Gomezes, the couple who run the souvenir shop next door, whisper to themselves. A few floppy-hatted tourists snap selfies nearby.

The tour bus blocks a good chunk of the street, so Karina politely shoulders her way past some tourists to get closer to the Fab Foodie Brothers. Elle and I stay close behind.

"I can't believe they're here," I say, texting my LA best friends, Molly and Carlos. We were in the Culinary Club together, and I even guest-hosted their YouTube cooking series sometimes. We also spent a month each summer at Kids Baking Camp, plotting the flashiest, tastiest group projects. The three of us were inseparable, at each other's houses, FaceTiming, or texting almost every second we weren't at school.

My heart pinches when I remember that they're at Kids Baking Camp now, cell phone–free.

I want that kind of close, anytime friendship here too, and the Seashell Squad sometimes makes me think I can have it. It's nice to be included in their hangouts and chats, but I worry they're only including that small, safe part of me I'm showing to the Coral Beach community, that they won't accept *all* of me. I haven't found any deeper sign that I can let my guard down and trust them the way I did my LA friends.

I feel like I'm just waiting for some sign from the universe that I can open up my whole non-cookie-cutter self, but no one's given me so much as a thumbs-up yet. I tuck my phone away and focus on the people around me.

Elle sighs. "Aren't they the best? Everyone's so jealous we're here." She's been sending pictures of the tour bus to the group Seashell Squad chat. My phone buzzes and I'm hopeful that it's Carlos or Molly, but it's only Elle's updates and emoji reactions from the other Seashells, Lane and Claire.

Elle's Fab Foodie Brothers fandom runs as deep as mine. During the school year, I was relieved to have something to talk about every Monday morning while our science teacher waited for his coffee to kick in. It was tricky keeping up with conversation about dance, choir, and other activities I'd missed out on because of our late-in-the-school-year move.

Someone bumps me from behind. The crowd is growing.

I scoot closer to Elle. "Did you see the episode where they rehabbed the Brazilian barbecue place? And they made it—"

"Vegan!" Elle laughs along with me.

Karina, on the tips of her toes, peers ahead. "I think they're about to start filming!" Then she wiggles her chiming phone out of her tiny jeans pocket. "That's our ballet teacher, Elle. We've gotta go."

Elle's posture deflates. "But the Fab Foodie Brothers!"

"Mom will kill me if I miss another class! Especially after how she paid to get *the* Ray Adair to do private lessons for us!"

Elle sighs. "Take some good pics, okay, Mila? I need all the details."

"I'm on it."

They weave their bikes out of the crowd, and I go in the opposite direction. Karina and Elle had invited me to join their ballet lessons. Even though it would've been great to have regularly scheduled hangouts with folks I'm trying to become better friends with, I declined. Ballet would eat up my time at the truck, and to be perfectly honest, I've got the gracefulness of a sleepy rhino. Right now, I'm thankful for a free afternoon. I'm nearly at the front of the crowd at a *Fab Foodie Brothers* show taping. I might even be on camera!

A man in a tight black T-shirt claps his hands to get our attention.

"Quiet, please! We're on in three, two . . ."

I push my back against the restaurant storefront to avoid a crew member rushing by. The new-paint smell wafts off the wall behind me, and I pray that it's dry.

Ahead, Chip Darlington smooths down his shirt, then flashes the gleaming, slightly lopsided grin I've seen on TV a thousand times. Next to him, Chaz, in pink, hooks his thumbs into the pockets of his pants, a pose that looks effortlessly casual, as if they just happened to wander by with a camera crew in tow.

"Hi, we're the Darlingtons—the Fab Foodie Brothers," they announce in unison.

My heart leaps. I suppress a cheer, which instead comes out as a low gurgle. One of the crew members throws a *be quiet* side-eye at me before turning back to the main attraction.

"We're here in gorgeous Coral Beach for the soft opening of our newest restaurant, Marigold and Myth!" Chip says. His voice is a note or two higher than his brother's, and his sapphire eyes sit closer together. Chip's the classically trained chef of the two. Chaz is the no-nonsense businessman with stellar design sense.

Delighted gasps and applause surround me, but they barely register against the roar in my ears. My idols, opening a restaurant here in boring old Coral Beach?

The Darlingtons smile at the crowd, and I swear I lock eyes with them.

Chaz speaks next. "This is a cutting-edge, top-secret concept that we've been dying to unveil. So join us tonight, live at seven, for a sneak peek at Marigold and Myth!"

Someone yells, "Cut!" and the din around me rises.

"We went to their restaurant in Beverly Hills. It's ten times better than anything I've had here. This is just what we need to kick-start Main Street again!" Mr. Gomez says from the souvenir shop.

My face crumples. Mr. and Mrs. Gomez are good friends of Grandma's (they go to the same Zumba Gold class), but I doubt they've tried the Banana Leaf's amazing fare.

I ignore Mr. Gomez and push toward the Darlingtons, hoping for a photo. I almost smack into one of their associates, a short, stocky Black man holding the waters. The pink of his shirt almost exactly matches the color of the Marigold and Myth doors, like he color-coordinated his outfit that way on purpose.

"Excuse me, the Darlingtons are very busy. No photos," he says, peering down at me through his round sunglasses.

I crane my neck to the left, trying to spot a way around this man, but the Darlingtons have already disappeared into the restaurant. Their other two associates guard the doors.

"The soft opening tonight," I say. "How do I get in?"

The man chuckles. "Sweetie, it's family and friends only." He says it in that roundabout way that automatically excludes me, the same way people said "We're having a party this weekend" or "Our car for the field trip is full" when I first arrived in Coral Beach.

"My name's not 'sweetie.' It's Mila."

He tips his head in acknowledgment. "Mila. I'm Gabriel. But that doesn't mean you're getting in here."

My shoulders slump, and his face softens. "Don't worry. The Darlingtons will be back in two weeks for the grand opening. You might be able to meet them then."

I nod as I'm bumped aside by a man carrying a potted plant. Nearby, the tourists flock into the Gomezes' shop to check out bird-shaped wind chimes. My phone buzzes with a message from the group chat: a picture of Karina and Elle in matching dance poses. I'm jostled until I stand at the edge of the sidewalk, trying to catch a glimpse of the Fab Foodie Brothers through the restaurant's curtained windows.

But somehow, even though I'm in the middle of the action, I feel left on the outside.

3

WHEN MY PHONE TIMER GOES OFF LATER that afternoon, I spring out of my room and head toward the kitchen. Calling it "my room" is a stretch: it's still very much Grandma's guest bedroom, complete with a rose-printed bedspread, fake roses in a white ceramic vase, and a cross-stitched wall hanging of—surprise, surprise— a rose. But by the window, there's a cheap desk and plastic chair that we brought from our old house. These, and the empty suitcase in the closet, are the only signs that our stay here isn't as temporary as we and Grandma had hoped it would be.

Dad works part-time at a renewable energy firm so he can spend the rest of his time on the food truck. We moved into Grandma's house partly because Dad needed the money to pursue his dream. Mom supported the idea even though she doesn't get along with Grandma. It was just for a little while, my parents said. But between Dad getting the truck up and running and Mom taking a break from work to care for her parents, it makes more sense for us to save on rent by staying with Grandma.

I peek into the oven to check my pandesal. They're starting to brown, and my mouth waters; I haven't had fresh Filipino bread since we left LA. Maybe I can convince Dad to do a limited-time-only sandwich at the truck using these rolls.

I'm running low on Catalina's Brightening Brew, so earlier I decided to re-create the potion myself while I waited for the pandesal dough to rise. Now, swirling the brownish-green liquid in a Coral Beach mug, I worry that the color is off. I don't think Catalina's instructions are the problem. I'm pretty sure it's me. I've never been able to create a potion on my own. That's why Catalina made so many for me before we left LA.

But there's only one way to test it. I pinch my nose, whisper "*Claritas*," and gulp down the unusually bitter blend of herbs.

My stomach gurgles, and I sprint to the bathroom mirror to see if there's the telltale glint of gold in my eye. I wait, but my plain brown eyes stare back at me, and I don't feel any brighter. All I've managed to conjure up is a slight stomachache and disappointment.

Back in the kitchen, I set the empty mug in the sink and check the clock on my phone: 5:03 p.m.

Speaking of disappointment: Mom said she'd call at four, or eight in the morning where she is in the Philippines, before she took Grandpa Ben to physical therapy. She missed our last video call too. We *did* trade texts with Catalina later that night, but it's not the same as speaking to her. Each text message ding reminds me that neither she nor my sister is here.

They would've been able to tell me where I went wrong with this brew. The albularyo skills are passed on through the women in Mom's family. But Mom and Catalina are much better at folk healing magic than I am, and Dad's no help. He always laughs that the only "magic" he can make is in the kitchen. I just don't understand how magic that runs so strong in my sister and mother could skip me entirely.

The back door swings open, and I start rinsing out the mug as Dad strolls in.

"Wow, that smells amazing," he says, sniffing the air dramatically. He has a smudge of black grime on his face from another DIY repair on the truck. "Baking? You asked Grandma if it's okay for you to cook, right?"

"Everyone loves the smell of fresh bread!" I say cheerily, hoping he doesn't realize I didn't answer his question.

Dad raises an eyebrow. "Mila, you know Grandma's got a certain way she likes things."

"I know," I mumble, lowering my gaze to the brown tile beneath us. "But didn't you say this is our home now too? Grandma's so intense about keeping this place spotless and rose-scented. She exploded when I microwaved that leftover fish burrito. I can't even use the truck's fryer because of some local health codes!" Though that hasn't stopped me from sneaking in now and then while Dad's off at his engineering job to attempt some potion brews.

"It *is* our home. But we still need to respect her rules."

"I don't have anywhere to test out new ideas, though."

Back in LA we had what we called a "dirty kitchen," an outdoor sink and stove for preparing our favorite smelly, messy, or, in my case, experimental foods. Grandma doesn't have the same setup because of Coral Beach laws, she says. How am I supposed to get Darlington-level culinary skills without practicing?

"We need to be on our best behavior with Grandma. We have to *try*. She's letting us stay with her, and we should be thankful."

I fold my arms across my chest. I *am* trying.

Dad tries to rub away a streak of dirt on his arm. "Once we get our own place, you can hang out in the kitchen all day, okay?"

Who knows when that will be? I think. But I force a smile for Dad. We've had this we're-moving-out-soon conversation so many times lately, yet we're still here.

Dad doesn't seem to believe my smile for a second, so he reaches out in the way he knows how. "You hungry?"

I nod. If Dad's determined to cheer me up, I'll let him. Particularly if it involves dessert. "Always. What'd you have in mind?"

"I think a dinner out is in order." Dad fishes for something in his back pocket just as Grandma walks in the front door.

She's back early from the salon; the chemical perfume wafting from her short, freshly dyed black hair proves it. "Eating out again? Shouldn't you be saving money?"

Dad frowns. "Ma. Not now."

Ignoring his warning, Grandma plants a hand on her hip. "You should be saving up, especially with Eva not working."

My heart squeezes at the mention of my mom. Grandma has always been hypercritical of her and Dad, and I don't want to hear anyone bad-mouth them.

Dad takes a step toward her, as if to shoo her away. "It's fine, Ma. It's one dinner. I saved us at least a hundred bucks by fixing the faucet leak in the food truck myself. And Eva will be back here—and back to work—any day now."

Grandma purses her lips. Right when I think she's going

to walk away, she takes a deep breath and narrows her eyes. "Mila! What did I say about using the kitchen?"

My head actually tilts in confusion. Everyone loves the smell of fresh bread, but it turns out we're staying with the one person who doesn't. I'm about to say so when a *be nice* eyebrow-raise from Dad douses my fire. "Um, sorry, Grandma. I'll clean up."

"Yes, you will," she says as she strides by me to slide open the kitchen windows. Then she takes a can of air freshener—rose-scented—from under the sink, sets it on the counter next to me, and walks off with a *hmph*.

Even with the windows open, this house feels more suffocating than before.

Dad sighs and turns back to me. "Once you clean up, get dressed. We're still going out for dinner."

My shoulders relax. "All right. The pandesal are ready to come out, anyway. Where were you thinking?"

"How about . . ." Dad's smile goes Cheshire Cat wide as he whips four strips of paper from his back pocket. "Marigold and Myth?"

My mood does such a rapid one-eighty that I get whiplash. I snatch the papers out of his hand, my fingers running over the gold-embossed restaurant name. "Soft opening tickets? How?"

He lifts his chin. "Carson Kent at the Chamber of

Commerce. The Darlingtons offered the chamber some courtesy tickets, and Carson figured Mr. Ram and I could use a look into how a brick-and-mortar restaurant starts up. Not that we're thinking of ditching the food truck, but I wasn't going to pass this up. Especially when you have such a big crush on those two."

"Dad!" My face goes red. "I do not have a crush. It is a professional admiration for their craft."

He laughs softly. "Either way, we get to admire them in person."

His nervousness from earlier, when we saw the buses and TV crews, comes to mind. "But are they our competition now? I mean, I love the Fab Foodie Brothers, but I love our truck more."

Dad waves his hand casually, but there's something else in his gaze. "Don't worry about that. Enjoy your brush with celebrity tonight. Now, we've gotta get moving. We're meeting Ram at the restaurant in an hour."

I hand the tickets back to Dad but frown as the math sinks in. "Who is the fourth ticket for?"

"You remember his nephew, Ajay, right?"

The name drags out a memory of us hanging out in LA a couple of summers ago. "Yeah! The kid we went to Disneyland with. He lives outside town, right?" More accurately, he lives on the far side of Coral Beach, in the exclusive gated community of Coral Bluffs.

"Yup. Ajay's dad got called to India for business unexpectedly, so Ram's helping to keep an eye on him for a couple weeks. I'm counting on you to show him how we run our truck."

The fact that Dad calls it *our* truck makes me smile. "Sure, I can do that."

Dad and Mr. Ram grew up together and ended up working at the same mechanical engineering firm in Los Angeles. Mr. Ram followed us up to Coral Beach. Having family nearby was a big reason Mr. Ram agreed to ditch his day job and move here to start the truck with Dad.

Mr. Ram is either the best friend ever or terrified that Dad's going to bungle everything. Maybe both. Adding his nephew may make the truck a little cramped, but to be honest, it'll be nice to see a familiar face in Coral Beach.

From what I remember, Ajay had a favorite Goofy shirt he wore twice in a row, an awe-inducing knowledge of Pokémon, and a love of cheese fries. Since he's new to the truck, he might have the perfect taste buds to help test out new recipes, like a Mila Special Pandesal Sandwich.

Dad brushes aside a pile of bills on the kitchen counter and sets the tickets in their place. "I'm going to wash this truck dirt off. We leave in fifteen minutes, okay?"

I arrange the tickets and snap an artsy picture to send

to Catalina just as the oven timer dings. I pull out a tray of perfectly pillowy golden pandesal. They look and smell delicious, but a taste will have to wait: I'm saving my appetite for tonight. Then I rush to my closet to dig out my fanciest of frocks: a flowy dress with tiny pink and brown donuts printed all over it.

I'm about to meet the two most important people in Cuisine Channel history. I need to look spectacular. Then I remember it's going to be televised live. I shoot out a quick text to Catalina and my LA friends, complete with the artsy picture of the tickets.

This is going to be the best night of my life.

4

I'VE NEVER SEEN THE TOWN SQUARE SO BUSY, not even when there are two cruise ships docked at the port. Shiny news vans line the streets. The sky is barely starting to pinken from the setting sun, so the searchlights perched on either side of Marigold and Myth's doors make the restaurant glow even more. A red carpet spills out of the storefront. Marigold and Myth looks like a mouth poised to gobble up customers.

I'm ready to be its prey.

I urge Dad to walk faster. We're fifteen minutes early, which almost never happens. People have already started lining up outside the restaurant. Something sweet and spicy perfumes the air.

Dad spots Mr. Ram first. "There he is!"

Mr. Ram, in a white button-down shirt and light gray slacks, looks more dapper than I've ever seen him. He even shaved what I thought was his permanent neck scruff. He waves us over, and Dad and I squeeze into line next to him. Thankfully, everyone is too busy on their phones to grumble at us for cutting in.

"Where's your nephew?" I glance around, looking for the gangly kid I remember.

Mr. Ram pokes at the shoulder of a tall boy in front of him. "How many times do I have to tell you to get off your phone, Ripley? Be polite."

"Wait, Ripley? I thought his name was Ajay."

At the sound of "Ajay," a kid three whole inches taller than me turns around.

The last time I saw him he was in that Goofy T-shirt, his super-short black hair covered by a dingy baseball cap. Today he's in a dark blue polo shirt, his puffy curls dusting a pair of black-framed designer glasses. He also wears a bomber jacket that's a couple of sizes too big for him, which is particularly weird because it's summer and eighty degrees out. I'm pretty sure his sneakers are the ones folks lined up for in the middle of winter too.

And here I am in a donut dress.

His glow-up makes me feel even more out of place in

Coral Beach. I wave, and his long-lashed brown eyes narrow, as if he's being expected to babysit instead of saying hi to an old friend.

Mr. Ram pokes him again. "You remember Mila, right?"

Ajay blows a breath out through his flared nostrils, sweeps a judgy gaze over my dress, then gives me a curt chin tilt. "Hi."

I'm too confused about the name switch to dwell on his bland greeting. "Hi, but is it Ripley or Ajay?"

"Ajay. Only my family calls me Ripley. It's an inside thing."

Of course it's an inside thing. All of Coral Beach seems to be in on things I'm clearly fenced out of. I smooth down my donut dress and Ajay returns his full attention to his phone.

Dad and Mr. Ram murmur to each other about Marigold and Myth. What kind of food are they serving? Is that cardamom they smell? I listen in on their hushed conversation. Ajay, meanwhile, has put in his earbuds and doesn't seem eager to talk.

"Hey, Mila!"

Elle waves at me from the front of the line, her pink bracelet sliding around her wrist. She and Karina are standing next to Karina's parents, who own a bed-and-breakfast near the water. Makes sense that the Fab Foodie Brothers would want the town's tourist draws to be present tonight.

"Come up here with us!" Karina shouts. She and Elle bunch together as if to make room for me.

If there's one thing I've learned about being friends with the Seashell Squad, it's that I have to be careful about turning down invitations. They're not as coldhearted as to shun me or anything; they didn't get angry that I didn't join Karina and Elle's ballet lessons. But I missed Claire's birthday party last month, and everyone is still cracking jokes I don't understand.

Coral Beach's biggest event of the year? They're going to be talking about this for months. I don't want to keep passing up opportunities to fully click into a group of people I like and who might like me back. Do I want to ditch Ajay (yes), Mr. Ram (not really), and Dad (definitely not) for Karina and Elle?

Suddenly, the line starts to move, taking the decision out of my hands.

"I'll see you in there," I yell back.

"You'd better!" Karina replies. "This is the best thing to happen to Coral Beach ever!" Then she and Elle disappear into the restaurant.

My heart leaps, trying to yank me inside faster. Someone has chalked bright, intricate rangoli around the walkway. I can barely contain the bounce in my step as we finally cross the threshold.

The inside is all bright whites and shimmery shades of orange and gold, with pops of the same pink and green as the exterior. Gold cloth is draped across the ceiling, giving the illusion that we're about to dine in some grand tent. The room smells of fresh paint and plastic wrap.

My fingers brush a marble fountain as someone takes us to our seats. In the middle of the small square table, a flickering candle floats in a vase of water. A sprinkling of fresh sampaguita and marigold blossoms surround the centerpiece.

Dad sits next to me, and he and Mr. Ram comment on the decor, how much the rent must cost, all that boring talk. I turn to Ajay to ask how his summer's been so far, but he's engrossed in carefully draping his bomber jacket on his chairback. There's a bulge in one of the jacket's pockets; he didn't bring his own snacks, did he? Who does that when dining at famous chefs' restaurants?

When he catches me squinting at his jacket, he glowers, plops down in his chair, and yanks out his phone. I don't know what I did to earn his standoffishness, but maybe with his slick haircut and designer everything, he's too Coral Beach cool to be seen with me.

Since no one else at my table wants to gush and Karina and Elle are seated at the far end of the dining room, I take out my own phone and snap a selfie.

Then the dining room erupts into applause as the Darlingtons exit the kitchen in bright white chef coats. The chef's whites are clearly just for show: there isn't a spot on them, so the Darlingtons can't be the ones actually cooking tonight.

The camera crew strafes the sides of the room, swinging lights and microphones around. They narrowly miss beaning Dad's chamber of commerce friend Mr. Kent.

Chip angles his face as if he knows exactly where the camera is and how to maximize his good side. "Welcome to Marigold and Myth! We're thrilled to have our closest friends and family, and of course you millions of viewers at home, join us in unveiling our newest concept."

I can practically feel Catalina's jealousy from her tiny apartment two hours away.

"We've spent months researching and honing our recipes. This exciting new fusion is going to put Coral Beach on the map! But simply talking about it would be boring, right?" Chaz pauses for some amused chattering. "Tonight, you, our guests, are going to guess which two countries are our inspirations."

On cue, waiters spill forth from the kitchen, gold platters on their hands. They march to each table and unveil the first course: three colorful plates and bowls full of appetizers meant to be shared.

"Countries as inspirations?" Ajay asks. His phone finally

sits facedown on the table, and all it took was the promise of food.

Dad and Mr. Ram are still speaking in low tones, so I fill him in. "The Fab Foodie Brothers are restaurant geniuses. They're especially well-known for their fusion concepts. They did a Japanese-inspired luxury ice cream shop at another beach town near LA. Think uni and gold flakes on a hot fudge sundae. It was a total hit. Won a ton of awards, and it became a celebrity favorite when one of the Avengers rented out the place for their kid's birthday."

A bit of awe must leak into my voice because Ajay nods matter-of-factly, like I'm a live Darlington book report.

Two waiters arrange the dishes on our table. On one glittery blue plate sit tiny stuffed puffs of fried pastry.

Mr. Ram's eyebrows knit. "Puri chaat?"

Something in my stomach twists, and I don't think it's from excitement. We serve a version of this Indian snack at the Banana Leaf, with Dad's own Filipino flare, of course.

"So Indian is one of the cuisines, then? What does that mean for us?" I ask.

Mr. Ram smooths a napkin down in his lap. "It might not mean anything. There are plenty of other ways they could have transformed this. It's worth a taste, isn't it?"

"Yaaarrrmm," Ajay moans, his plate empty and his mouth stuffed with chaat. "It'th tho good." He swallows.

"These Fab Food dudes know what they're doing."

I pick one up, excitement bubbling. Tailed by camera crews, the Darlingtons float from table to table, soaking up the compliments on live television.

I pop the chaat into my mouth, close my eyes, and let the flavors explode. When Mr. Ram first introduced these to Dad and me, he filled them with potato and topped them with yogurt and chutneys. Now I'm surprised by the tastes of pork belly, vinegar, and soy sauce. I catch a hint of liver, and the flavors begin to comfort me in an all-too-familiar way. It's when I taste the tang of citrus that my eyes fly open.

Dad watches me with wary curiosity.

I swallow. "Was that calamansi?"

Dad nods but doesn't say a word. He wipes his fingertips on his napkin.

"Wait, what'th calamanthi?" Ajay asks, still chewing.

"Calamansi is a type of Filipino citrus we use a lot in our Banana Leaf dishes. We get them straight from the tree my grandpa planted when he and Grandma moved here from San Diego."

I lick a dot of grease off my lips and frown. A popular Indian street snack of crispy fried bread stuffed with Filipino sisig, a chopped pork dish? The memory bursts out of my mouth. "This was the March special at the Banana Leaf!"

I don't know what it means that my culinary idols are

serving the same food Dad sells. The thought that they stole it flits across my mind, but these are celebrities. They wouldn't do that, would they? The flavors turn to ash in my mouth.

Dad shakes his head vigorously. "Quiet down, Mila, please."

"But it tastes exactly like your sisig puri, Dad!"

Ajay shrugs. "You said they're geniuses. Maybe they came up with it on their own."

The possibility sounds more reasonable coming out of Ajay's mouth. He's not a *Fab Foodie Brothers* superfan, nor is he invested in the Banana Leaf. But I still can't escape the unease in my chest.

Mr. Ram leans toward me, his voice low but hopeful. "We've only tried one thing. How about this other appetizer? It looks like a take on chips and dip."

I reach for a thin, brown chip at the same time he does and scoop up the light green sauce paired with it.

"The flavors are probably very different," Dad says.

"Yeah, maybe." I let some of the excitement creep back in again. Dad's combos are a hit: it was only a matter of time before someone else put the two cuisines together on their own too.

Still, even if their menu is different, a Filipino Indian celebrity restaurant is a huge threat to our Filipino Indian food truck. It doesn't matter that we got to Coral Beach first. No one's going to come to the Banana Leaf if they can get the same dishes—and a selfie at a celebrity joint—at Marigold and Myth.

I close my eyes and put the chip in my mouth. All at once I get crispy, salty, and coconutty, with fresh cilantro and a bite of spiciness from chilies.

I force a swallow before I turn to Dad. "Lumpia wrapper chips with cilantro-coconut chutney. That was—"

"On our menu when we first opened. I know," he says. He shares an unreadable look with Mr. Ram.

My mood drops. *Two* dishes can't be a coincidence.

On the table, my phone buzzes with messages from the Seashells group chat.

My parents said this is guaranteed to help business at the B&B!

These appetizers are AH-MAZ-ING

I hope they open 10 more restaurants in CB!

A waiter materializes next to me without a sound. He's a thin white man with a satiny pink vest over his black shirt. The only thing distinguishing him from the other staff is a dragon tattoo on his forearm. "Young lady, are these dishes not to your liking?"

Both Dad and Mr. Ram pin me with identical gazes that scream "play nice."

"They're delicious." The truth. Because they taste just like Dad's.

The dragon waiter chuckles like he doesn't believe me. I just want him to go away so I can ponder the threat to our family business. Yet somehow, the camera crew locks on me, the cranky kid who looks like she doesn't appreciate good food. One of the headsetted women points in my direction, and she and a cameraman move closer.

"Let me guess, you have a sweet tooth?" the waiter asks.

I nod just to get this conversation over with.

His face brightens. "Try this." He slides a tall, fuchsia-tinted glass of what looks like a smoothie in front of me. "It's our special lassi, a blend of yogurt, water—"

"I know what lassi is," I snap as I grab the glass. Under the table, Dad nudges my leg.

I take a sip. Cool yogurt, brown sugar, overripe banana, jackfruit.

I know this drink. I came up with it.

"No." I shake my head. "No, no, no."

"Oh wait, I forgot the best part!" the waiter says. He jams a triangle of crispy fried lumpia wrapper into my drink.

This is the Mila Special.

5

I SHOVE THE GLASS AWAY SO QUICKLY I knock it over, sending lassi splattering across Ajay and Mr. Ram. Mr. Ram leaps up, brushing the drink off his shirt, which just spreads the mess. A few drops have slopped onto Ajay's glasses.

"Cut to commercial!" someone yells, and the film crew fiddles with their equipment.

"Come on, Rip—Ajay. Let's get cleaned up. Your mom will kill me if I send you home like this," Mr. Ram says. Ajay barely has time to grab his bomber jacket before Mr. Ram yanks him toward the bathroom.

The dragon waiter snaps his fingers and suddenly three other staff members swarm in, rags and mops in hand.

Dad apologizes to them, then turns to me and says in a low voice only I can hear, "Mila, what was that about?"

"That's my drink! I invented it!"

He gives me a look so hard, his face could be made of stone. "You can't go accusing people of copying our recipes. Especially celebrities. And double-especially with all these cameras around." He forces a smile as if he suddenly remembers someone might be watching.

"Come on. What are the chances? Sisig puri? Lumpia wrapper chips and cilantro-coconut chutney? Turon lassi? I swear, if they have a ube gulab jamun . . ." The anger and lassi swirl like a storm in my stomach. I don't even think a couple of drops of Catalina's Rage Cage, a blend designed to calm anger, could reel in my feelings.

Then the film crew voice announces, "And we're back in three, two . . ."

I sense someone nearby and scoot in, thinking it's Mr. Ram and Ajay back from the bathroom. But to my surprise, it's none other than Chip Darlington.

"Everything all right here? It's our soft opening. We want to learn what we can do better."

My jaw almost hits the floor, and I have to remember to pick it up to answer. The gleam of Chip's eyes and smooth cadence of his words are wonders this close. I feel like I'm in a movie, a soot-covered villager gawking as the knight rides into town.

Which reminds me that we're being filmed. I sit up

straighter. Out of the corner of my eye, I see Dad trying his hardest to telepathically send me a message. *Behave.*

Why isn't he as ticked off as I am that their food tastes exactly like ours? I can always pretend that I didn't understand him. First, I have a couple of questions for the Darlingtons. (Though being so close to my longtime heroes douses some of the anger just a little.)

"These flavor combinations are so unique and creative. What inspired you?"

Chip grins as he pulls over his brother, who's been chatting with folks at a table nearby. "Actually, it was Chaz's idea. I know he's typically the design and business guy. But the idea of fusing Indian and Filipino flavors just came to him."

"Huh. Really. It just *came* to him."

Folding a giant slice of pizza to eat it just "comes" to someone. Fusing two complex, tradition-heavy, non-Western cuisines isn't that type of idea.

If Chaz picks up on my sarcasm, he doesn't mention it. He angles his face to the camera. "A mix-up of takeout orders one night. I knew the second I picked up some chicken adobo with hot, buttery paratha that our menu—"

"That's what *I* do," I blurt. That makes four dishes suspiciously like ours on the Marigold and Myth menu because of a supposed takeout mix-up. What are the chances?

Chip subtly tries to signal a director. Chaz scans the

room for another table—one with fewer pesky guests—to hop to next.

I feel guilty. The Fab Foodie Brothers are my heroes. They're the biggest thing I have in common with the Seashell Squad. I should be *grateful* the Darlingtons came to my new town, of all places.

But their restaurant might hurt ours because the concept is the same. Worse, this food tastes way too familiar to be a coincidence. Everything feels off, like a sugary dessert with a bitter aftertaste.

Chip chuckles, though I catch a trace of annoyance. "You do that too, eh? Great minds think alike." Then he and Chaz turn to the next table.

Their dismissiveness jabs at something raw in me. Maybe it's my missed call with Mom, or Grandma's off-limits kitchen, or the fact that I don't have any of Catalina's potions handy. But do I not deserve *anyone's* respect and attention for even a moment?

And what about Dad? He should have a place next to these celebrity chefs for his creativity.

I rise, brushing off the hand that Dad reaches out to stop me.

"Actually," I start to announce.

"Cut to a word from a sponsor, anything!" a woman snaps into her headset. Crew members flurry around her.

I ignore them and stand taller. "My dad is a great mind, too, because—"

"Mila—" Dad growls.

"Your food tastes just like his! We serve Filipino Indian fusion at our food truck, the Banana Leaf."

I sweep a hand to Dad then, expecting him to take credit. But the look of mortification on his face makes my hand drop. "Sit down, Mila!" he whispers harshly.

I don't understand why he's angry. I'm just trying to get everyone else to see that he's been cooking all this at the Banana Leaf for months.

Our corner of the restaurant suddenly feels too silent.

"Young lady, you should listen to your father," Chaz says. His words come out gently, but they're definitely an order.

I lower myself into my chair. Dad won't meet my gaze.

Then Chaz leans in, like he's talking only to me, even though he's still using a polished, on-camera voice. "I came up with this concept after a takeout mix-up when we were filming our Valentine's Day special. Now, it's wonderful that your father cooks something similar. Maybe we'll even check out your truck one day. Wouldn't that be fun?"

Before today, the Darlingtons eating at our truck would've been my dream. But now all I can manage is a weak nod.

"I can assure our guests that Marigold and Myth's

47

concept, the recipes—they're all original. We came up with them on our own, just like we do for the many Darlington establishments across the country." Chaz stretches out both arms like a ringmaster. "And you lovely people get to sample our cutting-edge cuisine tonight!"

Relieved applause fills the silence, as if people are more than happy to jump back into the delusion that everything's fine.

But I'm not. I'm about to question the Darlingtons again when Gabriel, the associate from earlier that day, blocks my view. "The rest of your party is outside," he says. "I suggest you join them."

Sure enough, Mr. Ram and Ajay are at the curb. Mr. Ram's dabbing at his shirt with a wad of paper towels, leaving lint everywhere. Ajay has his jacket back on and is tapping away on his phone.

Without a word, Dad heads for the exit and I follow. We pass by Karina and Elle's table on our way out, but they're so focused on arranging their plates for a pic that they don't notice.

The air outside feels chilly and stale. Dad waits until the doors close before turning to me. "Mila, I can't believe you did that."

I cross my arms. "Did what? I just asked them how they got their ideas! It's fishy, don't you think?"

"People come up with similar concepts all the time. You heard the guy's story."

"Concepts, I get. But exact recipes? Exact flavors? It's like they"—my heart breaks at the idea that I'm about to accuse my heroes of this—"*stole* them."

The Seashell Squad would hate me for even uttering those words. Especially Karina, with her parents' business standing to benefit from the extra tourists, and Elle, with her hearts-for-eyes looks whenever the Darlingtons are mentioned. Gushing about these celebrity chefs helped me start to fit in. Accusing them of stealing our recipes will alienate any potential friends for sure.

"We can't prove they did!" Dad lowers his voice when someone across the street glances our way. "You're the one who talks about how amazing these chefs are. You don't think it's possible they *created* some of these dishes like they said?"

My eyebrows scrunch. "It's possible, I guess. Unlikely, but possible." I begin to doubt my initial reaction. Maybe I did jump to a conclusion too fast.

Mr. Ram joins us then. "Are you two okay? What'd we miss?"

Dad catches him up, and for the first time since we left, Ajay glances up from his phone.

Mr. Ram sighs. "You have to admit this isn't good. We thought we could ride on the coattails of a celebrity presence, but not if they're serving the same cuisine."

"So maybe we talk to them, ask them to change their menu?" I suggest. "On TV, the Darlingtons seem like such nice guys. I'm sure if I explain, they'll see how much they're going to accidentally hurt a small local business."

"Not likely," Ajay cuts in. He whips his screen in front of my face. "Their team has been posting food pics on their social media accounts all night. Marigold and Myth is trending everywhere, and there are sixteen different livestreams from inside the restaurant. Those dudes aren't changing anything this popular."

I shake my head. If they understood what this food truck means to my dad, what it means to me, I know they'd budge. They had a holiday special where they bought a family a minivan after theirs was totaled during a Thanksgiving dinner delivery. There's no way guys like that would be coldhearted.

"I'll talk to them, they'll—"

"You'll do nothing like that," Dad says. His brow is tight and his shoulders look tense enough to snap like a rubber band. "You've already stirred up enough trouble. I'm going to have to apologize to them and to Carson from the chamber of commerce. You threatened a lot of connections tonight with your wild accusations."

"But Dad, we have to try. They can't take what's ours," I say.

Applause rings out from inside Marigold and Myth.

"Looks like they're already doing it." Dad fishes in his pocket for his keys. "Ram and I will find a way to smooth this over. Come on, let's go home."

"How about some burgers first?" Mr. Ram suggests. "Not like we got a full dinner in there."

They begin to walk to their cars as if that's the end of it. As if we're just going to roll over and let competitors—even celebrity ones—barge in on our hard-earned territory without a fight.

I grab Ajay by the arm. He looks at me like I've sprouted horns. "What do you want?"

"I want to protect our food truck," I say. "You want your uncle to succeed, right?"

"Of course. What kind of question is that?"

"Just making sure, because you didn't seem that interested in anything other than your phone and your stomach tonight. If you're going to be hanging around with us for the next few weeks, you've got to pull your weight."

Ajay shoves his hands into his pockets. "Look, Ram Uncle threw all his money into the Banana Leaf. My mom's really mad about it. But my uncle looks happy. Much happier than when he was stuck in an office. So yeah, I'm up for helping him and your dad."

With a pinch of sadness I realize that's the most he's said

to me today. My whole night got twisted around. I expected a reunion with a friend and was met with someone who preferred his phone to me. I expected to gush over my chef heroes only to learn they might ruin us. And I expected to be full, but my stomach grumbles so loudly I have to cough to cover up the noise. At least Dad and Mr. Ram are going to fix the hunger problem.

"We can hammer out a plan at the truck tomorrow," I say. When Ajay's lips purse like he's bitten into a lemon, I add, "Hey, working at the Banana Leaf isn't that bad. Juggling everything during the lunch rush can sometimes be fun."

He shakes his head. "Going to India with my dad was supposed to be fun. He didn't have time to take me around during his business trip, though."

Ajay sighs in a way I recognize well. I feel the same about Mom being overseas. I'd hoped I could go with her instead of staying in Coral Beach for the summer. I could've met more of Mom's side of the family, learned about where we come from, maybe even tried brewing my own potions with her help. But the fact that the school year wasn't over gave Mom an easy excuse to leave me in Coral Beach.

Ajay seems determined to have a bad time at the Banana Leaf, but maybe I can cheer him up. I reach into my messenger bag, feeling for the nearly empty bottle of Brightening

Brew. "I have something that might help. It helped with that icky feeling when my mom went on a long trip too. My sister brewed it."

Ajay raises an eyebrow. "Catalina? I remember her driving us to Disneyland. She had those healing books and plants in the back seat."

The memory flits to the top of my mind, like the last warm note of a spice. "Yup, that's her. She's been training to become an albularyo, a type of Filipino folk healer."

"Is this one of her potions?"

When I nod, he agrees to try it. I know from Mr. Ram that, like in the Philippines, a lot of folks from India and plenty of other countries more easily blend the everyday and the mystical. It's not unusual for Western medicine and folk healing methods, or science and mythology, to coexist harmoniously. Mr. Ram would rather sip ginger peppercorn milk tea than reach for cold medicine, and we've got both a Ganesha statuette and an Our Lady of Manaoag scapular on the Banana Leaf dashboard. I don't have to convince Ajay that magic exists.

"*Claritas*," I whisper as he places a couple of drops on his tongue.

"Is that Latin?" Ajay says. "Did you know Latin is still one of the official languages of Vatican City?"

I don't know how to respond to that. "Um, cool, I guess.

Let me know if you feel the potion working."

"How will I know?"

"It varies. Sometimes people burp. My dad says his toes start to tingle."

"Oh! Here we go. My toes are—" Ajay burps. Then gold flashes across his eyes, his brow relaxes, and some of that Coral Bluffs too-coolness seems to melt away.

"Wow," he whispers. "It's like my brain only wants to focus on the good stuff now. Dad was supposed to be home this summer. We had plans to go snorkeling and drive up to the bay, before his unexpected business trip killed all that. And somehow he assumed me tagging along would be too much trouble. But . . . now all I can think of is how much fun we're going to have when he gets back."

I smile. That's how the Brightening Brew is supposed to work. It lets you see the rays of sunshine through the clouds. I suppress a pang of disappointment at my failed attempt to brew a new batch myself.

Mr. Ram's voice drifts back to us. "Hurry up, you two!"

"Not a word about the potion to them, okay?" I tell Ajay.

"Why? Is it illegal or something?"

"No, nothing like that. But I've used it to help customers at the truck a few times, and Dad and Mr. Ram wouldn't approve of me doctoring our food. I swear it's always been for a good cause."

"Got it. But you've got to do something for me too."

I almost stumble. What do I have to offer? I can't even brew these potions myself!

"Throw away that donut dress. It's a little tacky."

My jaw drops. "Are you serious? It's my favorite!"

"It makes you look like a little kid. And I have to be seen with you for the next couple weeks!"

I glare at him. Is that why he was rude to me earlier? I glance down at my beloved donut dress.

"I'm not throwing it out," I grumble. "But I'll pack it away while you're with us." It's a small price to pay to keep this secret from Dad and Mr. Ram.

Ajay, surprise fashionisto, gives me a smug nod.

"In fact, I'll even stop wearing the matching donut scrunchie and socks if you help with this whole Marigold and Myth business, especially since Dad and Mr. Ram don't even want to talk about it."

"Yuck, there's a scrunchie too? Deal accepted, of course. What can I do?"

I think of the phone that's practically been welded to Ajay's palm all night. "So, you follow the Fab Foodie Brothers on Instagram?"

6

THE WHOLE NIGHT, MY PHONE RUMBLES WITH Seashell Squad group chat texts.

I swear, Chaz looked right at me!

There's a crew after-party at the bar next to the B&B! Mom's thrilled. Not even going to complain about the noise.

Karina, how about an impromptu sleepover at the B&B? We can all camp out and wait for celeb sightings!

Do you think Chaz would remember me?

A dozen times, I start to type out a message about my suspicions. But then I erase it, thumbs-up everyone else's texts, and take yet another bite of pandesal. I don't want to be the one spoiling everyone's fun. Karina and Elle must've been so wrapped up in the excitement of the soft opening that they didn't notice I left before the main course.

That doesn't mean I'm not going to get to the bottom

of this, though. Earlier, as we waited for our burger orders, Ajay and I learned two things from the Fab Foodie Brothers' official social media accounts.

First, I counted at least six of the Banana Leaf's bestselling items on Marigold and Myth's limited opening menu. From reading the dish descriptions, it looks like they just ran our menu copy through a thesaurus app. We call something tasty? Theirs is delectable.

Second, the Darlingtons are staying in town two more days to finish up business and get to know the locals. That explains the after-party. They want to show that they're going to be an economic blessing to this community. Then they won't be back until before the grand opening, the weekend after next.

One of their other stops will be Elle's sister's salon, A Cut Above the Rest. The only reason I know this is Elle's message: **SILVER IS TRIMMING CHIP'S AND CHAZ'S HAIR TOMORROW! CATCH ME, I'M FAINTING.**

This is my chance to speak with them.

The next morning, my messenger bag bumps against my hip as I speed walk toward A Cut Above the Rest. Ajay is close on my heels. I guzzle down the pineapple-banana smoothie I made for myself and Dad this morning.

My smoothie is laced with Catalina's MettleMix, a special elixir to inspire bravery. She only gave me two bottles for when I started at Coral Beach Academy, in case I had trouble working up the nerve to talk to people. The supply was supposed to last me a year. Even at only a couple of drops per dose, I finished the first bottle in a month. I've had to carefully ration the second one.

Silver squeezed in an appointment for me at 10:15 a.m. in exchange for a 10 percent off coupon at our truck. Thanks to trouble with Grandma's Stone Age printer—and Ajay demanding I not wear my "tacky" taco earrings—we're running late.

Ajay's so focused on his phone that he's nearly walked into two trash cans. He's in his oversize bomber jacket again, but at least he had the warm-weather instinct to wear shorts today.

"Catching them mid-haircut seems like a bad idea," he says.

"I need to figure out what's going on. And without cameras around, maybe they'll be more likely to talk."

"It's worth a shot, I guess. They didn't answer our Instagram DMs."

I shake my head. Maybe the Darlingtons aren't responding because they have something to hide.

The bells above the door chime as I enter. The salon is all silver and black, with a few fake plants and pops of pink here and there. A scissors-shaped neon-pink sign buzzes on one wall.

I hear Silver before I see her. "Welcome! Be with you in a second."

I peek around a fake Swiss cheese plant and Silver comes into view. She's tall and lean, her cropped hair dyed an edgy gray that shimmers against her pale, pink-toned skin. A black apron covers her fuzzy candy-heart-pink sweater and cutoffs, and she's forearm-deep in a storage cabinet toward the back of the salon.

My heart skips when I see that the Fab Foodie Brothers are occupying two styling stations. One reads a magazine, the other chats on his phone. And in a styling station nearby is none other than Elle, who is obviously trying to take selfies with them in the background.

I freeze. I had planned on having a polite conversation with the Darlingtons about their restaurant. Then I'd ask whether they'd pretty please reconsider their concept. It's going to be tough to do around Elle, who might let slip in the group chat that I'm pestering everyone's favorite celebrity chefs. My resolve wavers, even with the hefty dose of Mettle-Mix. I take a step back, only to bump into Ajay.

"Careful!" he says, looking me in the eye for the first time today.

"We . . . we should go," I whisper. I try to weave around him to head out the door.

"It was your idea to—"

"Mila? Is that you?" Elle's voice sails over the lo-fi music streaming out of a speaker in the corner.

I whip around and throw a smile at her. "Hey! Didn't see you there! That station open?" I point toward a vacant leather chair.

"Yeah, let me grab you a cape. You want a cucumber water?"

"Um, sure."

"Make it two waters," Ajay cuts in.

"This is Ajay," I say, casting Elle an apologetic look for Ajay's rudeness. "He's helping at the truck this summer."

"Did you know cucumbers are ninety-five percent water?" Ajay says. "You're basically serving water water with a hint of cucumber."

"Cool?" Elle says with a confused but kind smile. "I'm Elle."

"I thought you were supposed to be helping out at your dad's fishing equipment rental shack this week," I say.

"Came in special for you-know-who's visit! Now, let me get you those drinks."

To Elle's credit, she's certainly trying to make a show of being useful. The floor is spotless. I seat myself at the styling station and stash my bag next to me. My chair squeaks as I rotate to spy on the Darlingtons. Ajay drags a metal stool over from nearby.

"So are you just here to bother them or are you really going to get a haircut?" he asks. "Because I have some ideas for your hair so you don't look so much like a six-year-old."

I shush him. "I'm going to talk to them. I'm just . . ." Still starstruck? Intimidated? Terrified I'm going to ruin my friendships for possibly nothing? ". . . trying to find the right moment."

The stylist next to the Darlingtons pulls off a gooey pair of latex gloves and heads into the back room.

"Go," Ajay whispers. "They're literally stuck in chairs with goo in their hair. You won't find a better time."

"*Fortiter et fideliter*," I mumble to myself: the incantation for the MettleMix. I struggled through the pronunciation earlier, when I first added the drops to my smoothie, and I don't know if saying it again will somehow renew it. But right now I'll take all the bravery—magical or not—I can get.

"You know, one of the earliest forms of hair gel was a fat-based product used by ancient Egyptians as far back as three hundred BC," Ajay offers.

"Not now, Ajay," I say as I rise from my chair. The sound of my steps is drowned out by the thumping of my heart.

I cough to get their attention. Chip sets down his magazine. Surprise, then annoyance, flits across his face before his on-camera smile replaces it. "You, from the soft opening last night."

I smile. "Hi. I think we got off on the wrong foot. I'm Mila."

At that, Chaz looks at me, then mumbles an "I've gotta go" to whoever's on his phone. "Well, Mila, are you here to apologize?"

"Y-yes. Sorry for the mess." Which is true. I feel bad that I not only ruined Mr. Ram's shirt, but that their staff had to clean up after me. I know how sticky that job can be.

"No apology necessary," Chip says, returning my smile. "We just hope you enjoyed the food."

"I did. I just . . . um . . ." I have their attention, but the words are stuck like melted hard candy on the pavement.

"Yes? How can we be of service to you, Miss Mila?" Chaz leans toward me in encouragement. He has this ease about him that inspires me to open up. This must be why he's so good at the business side; an hour with him, and people are probably signing over their whole restaurants.

"We . . . I think . . . um . . . Is there any way you could serve something else at Marigold and Myth? Please. We've already got amazing Filipino Indian food at my family's food truck. Don't get me wrong, I'm a huge fan of your show. But

I'm a little worried about having two places in town serving the same food."

The Darlingtons laugh until they realize I'm not smiling. I glance behind me, and Ajay looks just as serious. He nods.

"Oh, you're serious," Chaz says to me. "Well, kiddo, I hate to disappoint a fan, but we simply can't do what you're asking. We've invested a lot of time and money into Marigold and Myth. We'll just have to learn to live together."

I shake my head. Maybe I'm not being clear, but talking to my longtime culinary idols is daunting. "But that's the problem. A hawk will always say that to the mouse before it gobbles it up anyway."

"Mila, what are you doing?" Elle stands next to Ajay, two plastic cups of cucumber water clenched tightly in her hands.

Sorry, I mouth at her, before turning to the Darlingtons again. "What I'm trying to say is that your restaurant might take all our customers. The food's just so similar that no one's going to want to come to the Banana Leaf, and that truck is my dad's world. You understand, right?"

The brothers sigh and exchange a look I can't decipher.

"That's business, kiddo," Chaz says with a shrug.

My heart sinks. The wrinkle between Chip's eyebrows makes him look truly apologetic, but he doesn't say a word.

Then Ajay's voice booms next to me. "Then what do you

63

have to say about the food being *exactly* like the Banana Leaf's?"

Ajay has his phone out and is taking video. I thought it was a good idea to bring him along for moral support, but I didn't envision him accosting the Darlingtons paparazzi-style.

I let out a laugh, trying to ease the awkwardness by pretending this is all a lighthearted joke. But the sight of the phone instantly wipes the informality off the Fab Foodie Brothers' faces. Their perfect TV smiles flash on like lightbulbs.

"My brother came up with those recipes himself," Chip says. "It must be a coincidence."

My pulse starts to race. "That's what I thought at first, but my taste buds don't lie, and the flavors are too similar to be an accident."

Dad's adobo tastes different than Mom's. Mr. Ram uses more cardamom in his chai than his sisters do, and he's very precise about the salt in his chutney. The chances of Chaz coming up with the exact same flavors for the dishes we tried—complete with that zing of exactly one and a half calamansi—is near impossible.

Plus, Chaz isn't a trained chef like his brother. If he came up with the idea, how did he magically create these recipes my dad spent half a lifetime perfecting? He had to have had help. Either Chip is lying to make his brother look good, or they've got a whole team somewhere doing their dirty work.

I didn't expect the Darlingtons to dig in their heels like this, and I know Dad would tell me to let it go. He'll probably work harder to cultivate new recipes or customers. But that means him dedicating more time and money trying to keep the truck afloat, which means less of both at home. We'll be at Grandma's forever.

Near Ajay, Elle's jaw hangs open. I hope I can apologize to her later so she'll think this was just a momentary lapse in judgment.

"What exactly are you implying, kiddo?" Chaz says, an edge to his voice.

I push my shoulders back, stand up straight, and throw my worst-case-scenario theory out into the world. Unfortunately, my voice wavers. "I—I think you stole the Banana Leaf's recipes."

Chaz raises an eyebrow. "Did you actually accuse *me* of stealing?"

Ajay swings his camera at me to catch my reaction.

"I . . . I guess I did."

Chaz lets out a huff through his nose. "Excuse me." He raises his voice to get the attention of anyone but us. "Can someone please collect these children?"

"Children?" Ajay chokes out.

Chip smiles straight at Ajay's camera. "We appreciate our fans, but this is too much. We deserve some privacy."

Ajay takes a step toward them. "Then say straight-out that you didn't steal the recipes, and we'll leave you alone. Swear it."

"We don't have to answer to you. Turn that thing off," Chaz growls.

Out of nowhere, Silver and the other stylist appear. "Our apologies, Mr. Darlington. We'll take care of this," Silver says, before whirling around to glare at her sister. "Elle, get your little friends out of here."

I'm about to mention that I have an appointment, but then I remember I don't actually have sixty-five dollars to spend on a cut I don't need. I let Elle usher Ajay and me outside.

Ajay tucks his phone carefully into his jacket. "We can watch the footage later, look for any tics, body language showing nervousness."

I do a double take. "What? How do you know to do all that?"

Ajay smirks. "I've been marathoning detective shows. You and your wardrobe are so lucky I'm stuck with Ram Uncle this summer, Mila."

Elle groans. "Is that what you two are doing? Some big sting operation?"

I wince at her tone.

"I'm so sorry, Elle. I didn't mean to get your sister in trouble, but—"

Elle leans in. "Because I didn't want to say anything, but their turon lassi? An exact copy of the one I get from the Banana Leaf!"

My shocked laughter comes out shaky. "Wow, I must be onto something if it can turn another devoted fan into a doubter."

Elle shrugs. "Well, they didn't need to tattle on you to Silver. I thought they were amazing, but it's not cool if they really are trying to tank your dad's business."

"Thanks for understanding," I say sincerely, even though I don't miss that hint of doubt in her voice. She's not ready to cast the Fab Foodie Brothers as villains.

Elle continues, "You know, I can't even imagine what I'd do if some big fishing equipment rental corporation set up shop next to my dad's shack."

"I . . ." Are there even big fishing equipment rental corporation villains out there? "Yeah. It's scary to think they could wipe out everything my family's built."

"And that Ram Uncle's built too," Ajay adds. "We still need answers."

I peer back at the closed door of A Cut Above the Rest. "They wouldn't even swear they didn't steal our ideas. I need more evidence."

"Can we wait for them to leave and bug them more then?" Ajay asks. "Or figure out where they're going next?"

"I . . . I don't know, Mila," Elle says, her eyes on the ground. "I agree something is fishy about how Chip and Chaz wouldn't answer you. I've watched enough of their shows and specials—sometimes twice—to know that that's not their normal style. But Silver won't want me messing with her clients. And my mom loves the Darlingtons so much . . ."

I try to ignore the tightness in my chest at Elle's hesitation. "I know you're a huge fan too," I offer as a way out.

"All of us are," she says. She's right, and I fill in the words she doesn't say: going against the Darlingtons means going against the Seashells and practically everybody in Coral Beach. Elle does sound like she believes me, but I couldn't have expected her to side with me against everyone, could I?

Still, I'd be lying if I said it didn't sting. "Maybe I'm wrong. But we'll get to the bottom of this."

"Of course we will, like the bottom of a french fry cup," Ajay chimes in. "Um, Mila, that is not a suggestion for you to go out and buy some french-fry-print clothes."

I glare at him, but it's nice to have someone on my side.

"Don't worry, Elle. We'll stay out of Silver's salon." I pluck the Banana Leaf coupon out of my pocket and hand it to her. "Can you give this to your sister as an 'I'm sorry' from me?"

After she takes it, my shoulders slump. "Well, this was a bust," I say. "We still somehow have to find proof that the Fab Foodie Brothers stole the Banana Leaf's recipes."

"But once we have it, we'll spread the word," Ajay says, waving his phone at me. Dad won't let me access social media anything, yet Ajay somehow has his own account on every app. "And voilà, their restaurant is out of Coral Beach. We expose the Darlingtons for who they are and save the Banana Leaf and Ram Uncle's savings."

He makes it sound easy, even though I know it won't be. "Let's not mention our salon visit to Dad or Mr. Ram. Dad will flip out."

"I can cover for you. But first," Elle says, "can you take your cucumber waters? I've been holding them for like ten minutes."

7

WE RETREAT TO ELLE'S FAMILY'S BUNGALOW to plan. She brings out three forks and half a pie tin of her sister's Dutch crumb apple pie. Sugar is exactly what my brain needs.

We set up faded fabric beach chairs around a wooden table, grab forks, and dig in. Ajay chews while he watches the video he recorded earlier.

I take my first bite of pie and nearly melt out of my seat. "Elle, your sister makes the best Dutch crumb apple in the world."

Across from me, Ajay slips a hunk of piecrust into his jacket pocket without taking his eyes off his screen. He must love this pie as much as I do.

Elle lifts her chin an inch as she smiles. "I'll let Silver know. Maybe she'll forgive you for bugging her clients."

"Then I hope she can forgive me for trying to drive them out of town."

Elle shrugs. "She'll get over it. Don't tell anyone, but deep down, she's a softy. She's all about the little guy. If you prove that what you're saying is true, she'll hate the Darlingtons for stealing your dad's hard work. Those are his recipes, right?"

"They are. Well, actually, I came up with the turon lassi. My mom makes the best turon. I could eat like a dozen in one sitting."

I hope she doesn't notice the wobbling of my voice at the mention of my mom. If Mom were here, she'd believe me, I know it. But she's not, and she doesn't have a return ticket yet. By the time she gets back, Marigold and Myth will be up and running and stealing all our business.

"I don't think I've had too-rone," Elle says, trying her best to shape her English-molded tongue to Filipino sounds. "You know, I don't think I've seen much Filipino food outside of your dad's truck. You never bring any to school."

Which is purposeful. I already have a hard enough time fitting into Coral Beach Academy and the Seashell Squad. Whipping out Filipino favorites like chocolate meat (don't knock it until you've tried it, but hint: it's not really chocolate) and propping my leg up on the seat at lunch like I do at home? People say they welcome differences, but they're also quick to whisper snarkily about them.

But that's too much to unload on Elle right now. She eats at the Banana Leaf, so strong, rich smells and flavors aren't foreign to her. But explaining how I bring turkey sandwiches and prepackaged bags of chips—when my dad is a talented chef—because I'm trying to belong? I'm not ready to have that conversation with myself, let alone her. I'm still figuring out what kind of world I'm trying to belong *to*.

My sister would get on my case for not being proud to be Filipino American. Easy for her to say, when she's still surrounded by Filipino American friends and folks who don't look twice at a new brown kid. It's hard to be brave alone sometimes, which is why when school started, I practically guzzled down my limited stash of Catalina's MettleMix.

Ajay rescues me from my thoughts by jutting his phone between Elle and me. "Those Fab Foodie Brothers look totally guilty."

I squint. "They look how they usually do."

"But see how often they're blinking? It's like their eyelids are racing." He angles the phone so I can see it better. "I picked that tip up from a true crime documentary on channel seven."

I don't see exactly what he's seeing, but his comment gives me an idea. "That's it! The Channel Seven Sleuths! 'Tamra Wells is on your side, investigating and fighting for you'!"

72

Elle toys with the seashell on her bracelet while she thinks. "That's not a bad idea, Mila. If there's really something wrong, then Tamra Wells will know what to do. She helped that elderly couple get their roof fixed after the contractor stopped showing up! She tracked him all the way to Fresno and got him to repair everything for free. And if you're wrong, at least the Darlingtons won't blame the investigating on you."

I lean back in my chair, a growing smile on my face. "Tamra Wells will figure out the truth. I know it."

"Sorry, kids. Can't help you."

Tamra Wells shakes her head. Sun glints off her black ringlet curls and the turquoise eyeglass frames that pop against her dark brown skin. She takes a sip of her cold-brew coffee, leaving a magenta lip mark on the plastic cup. Then she pulls out a mirror to check her flawless makeup. She's paying more attention to her lipstick than to the two kids standing next to her.

Ajay and I staked out her regular outdoor table at the café outside Channel 7 Studios. Ajay analyzed Tamra's location tags and daily posting habits and pinpointed this place.

We caught the trolley here with our free student passes. Elle went back to A Cut Above the Rest to smooth things over with Silver so she wouldn't blab to my dad about my chat with the Darlingtons.

I don't know how much help I'll ask Elle for anyway. Every pause in her words, every glance away, told me she wasn't sure if she should believe me. Something in her was fighting to retreat back to what she knew—that the Fab Foodies were the best!—and fall in line.

The Banana Leaf and I don't have the luxury of that option.

I cough to get Tamra to focus. "But why not? You're always helping regular citizens right wrongs, aren't you? That's exactly what I'm asking you to do here."

She snaps her compact mirror shut. "Let me get this straight. You want me to take on Chip and Chaz Darlington." She enunciates their names so precisely, it's like she's separating each syllable with a sharp knife. "Cuisine Channel's multimillion-dollar-making sweethearts. The ones whose restaurant is supposed to bring in a boatload of tourist money and lift the town out of its economic rut. That's who you want me to go up against?"

"Yup."

She sighs and takes another sip of cold brew.

"Look, your story is compelling, Mila, but this kind of investigation is going to make a lot of people unhappy. A lot of people, including my bosses. You hear me?"

Ajay crosses his arms. "So you're all about helping the little guy unless it means risking your career."

A small smile flits across her face. "Smart kid. You'll understand this one day." The smile drops and she gives a long, tired exhale that seems at odds with the massive amount of caffeine she's ingesting. "Look. I'm the first Black anchorwoman with her own segment on this station, and I fought hard to get here. So I'm going to need a lot more than hunches and dodgy answers. Come back to me when you've got something solid, something my bosses can't ignore. But until then? I can't help you. I'm so sorry."

Tamra's apology is sincere, but it doesn't matter. Our one hope for relentless, thorough, televised investigation picks up her belongings and heads into the studio.

"Are there any other news teams we can run this by?" Ajay asks.

I swallow hard. "Yeah, but they're probably going to give us the same answer. No one's going to believe two kids with a hunch."

We trolley back to the truck in time to help with the lunch rush. But to my surprise, there isn't the usual line in front of the serving window. Instead, there's a red-haired white man in dark aviator sunglasses, a collared short-sleeved shirt, and tie. He wields a pen and a clipboard almost menacingly, like a sword and shield. A badge hanging from a lanyard around his neck reads *Inspector, Coral Beach Department of Environmental Health.*

I almost stumble over my own feet. "A surprise health inspection?"

Dad spots me and Ajay, and though he waves, his face stays grim. "Nothing to worry about, kids. Mr. Reynolds here is only doing a routine check—"

"Due to an anonymous complaint," the mustached Mr. Reynolds finishes. "Just called in. Unsanitary conditions. Maybe even cockroaches or rats in or around the truck." He waves his pen, as if pointing to these phantom pests.

Ajay starts to cough, then lifts his elbow to stifle the noise. He must be reading my mind: What are the chances that this surprise health inspection is due to me asking too many questions of our town's new big-time chefs?

I stay quiet as Dad and Mr. Ram follow Mr. Reynolds around the truck. This must be why Dad didn't want me to make a scene. No one in Coral Beach wants to drive the Fab Foodie Brothers and their money away. My meddling could result in backlash against our truck. Like an anonymous false complaint that brings the health inspector to our door.

Not that the health inspector will find anything to cite us for. But it's not good business to have him poking around at lunch hour.

I tug Ajay off to the side. "About the rat . . . ," he begins.

"There are no rats in our truck!" I snap. I massage my temples, wishing I'd brought a bottle of Catalina's Rage

Cage with me, then plant my hands on my hips and glare at Mr. Reynolds. He kicks at the front tire of the Banana Leaf, as if it's full of critters.

"Looks like you'll need some new tires soon, too," Mr. Reynolds says, scribbling on his clipboard.

Mr. Ram drags a hand through his hair. "That'll be another thousand dollars, probably," he says, exchanging a worried glance with Dad.

I gulp, then turn to Ajay. "I think someone's trying to scare us off, keep us from bugging the Fab Foodie Brothers. You heard Tamra. To save the Banana Leaf, we need hard proof that the Darlingtons stole from us."

"What kind of proof?"

"I'm not sure," I say, as Dad casts a pursed-lip glance in my direction. He won't say out loud that he blames me for this sudden health inspection, but I feel a squeeze of guilt anyway. He can't even fight back because he needs the city officials on our side. "But I am sure we're going to have to get it ourselves. We can't rely on anyone else." Especially not the adults.

8

THE NEXT DAY, AJAY AND I LURK AT THE
entrance to the alley behind Marigold and Myth and
spy on the moving crew trudging in and out of its back
doors. With less than two weeks until the grand opening, it
looks like they're making the decorations even brighter and
more glittery than before.

Thanks to Elle's eavesdropping during the Darlingtons'
salon session, we know the brothers are shooting some meet-
and-greet luncheon with the mayor at city hall today. But
apparently that doesn't mean the restaurant will sit empty,
as I'd hoped.

"The extra art will look better in photos," Ajay says. "And
a whole orchid wall? Influencers are going to eat that up."

I grimace. "Whose side are you on?"

"The side of art, obviously," Ajay says with a dramatic

brush of his short black curls. "Anyway, we have to know our enemy, right? From the looks of it, our enemy is going all out to make Marigold and Myth a destination."

Not if I can prove they stole our recipes. "Come on, they're finally starting to head out for lunch. Now's our chance."

It's Friday, which means Dad and Mr. Ram are doing a shorter lunch service to prepare for tonight's big Concert in the Park gig. It's our biggest-selling night, so we need to rest up.

Ajay and I helped with as much prep as we could before begging out for some time at today's Coral Beach craft fair. Mr. Ram thought it was a great idea and even gave us spending money. He probably wouldn't approve of us crafting a takedown plan in the alley behind Marigold and Myth.

Ajay stashes his phone into his jacket pocket, and we squat-run video-game-style to a spot hidden by a dumpster. A trailer full of crates blocks the other end of the alley. Three of the five-person moving crew left for a break five minutes ago. Two men are still inside the trailer, arguing about who is going to lift a heavy brass elephant statue.

I inch around the dumpster toward the open door. Ajay and I slip into the restaurant as the men in the trailer start playing rock, paper, scissors.

The empty kitchen gleams with spotless stainless steel.

The white walls are lined with shelves of shining pots, pans, and dinnerware, and a rainbow of condiment bottles glows above one countertop. Warm lights illuminate the whole room.

I take a moment to appreciate the open space. I love the Banana Leaf, but it's cramped with Dad and Mr. Ram cooking and me manning the register.

Ajay taps me on the arm. "There, the office." He points to a room in the corner, its door slightly ajar, and we pad toward it. The room seems to be dark, silent, and (hopefully) unoccupied.

I push the door open with my fingertips. The place is so polished that the hinges don't even creak. Ajay and I scurry inside. He sets his phone on flashlight mode, and two matching desks, brown leather chairs, and nearly empty bookcase come into view.

"No computer? Not even a tablet?" Ajay whispers.

I frown. I don't doubt that Ajay would've found a way to hack into a password-protected anything. Searching drawers and flipping through papers is going to take longer, and the rest of the moving crew may return from lunch soon.

"I'll take the desks," I say, putting my own phone on flashlight mode. "You take the bookcase."

I pick one desk and tug open the top drawer but find only pens, highlighters, paper clips, and Post-its. The next drawer holds some blank leather-bound notebooks. The bottom drawer is locked.

No one uses a lock unless they have something to hide.

"Help me with this," I whisper to Ajay. "Maybe we can pull it open?"

"Stand aside," he says, cracking his knuckles. Taking a paper clip from the top drawer, he wriggles it around in the lock. There's a tiny click, and Ajay pockets the paper clip. "Now help me pull on the count of three."

On three, I pull my hardest. Something catches my wrist, but the drawer flies loose. I land flat on my butt, holding the drawer in both arms.

Ajay shines his phone flashlight into the drawer as I flip through the file folders. A leasing agreement, a filming schedule, release forms for their TV show, but no recipes. Not even any purchase orders for ingredients. All the paperwork dates from the past two months. I keep thumbing through, but there's no master plan to steal from the Banana Leaf in here.

With every piece of paper, my doubt grows. Maybe I'm wrong about the Fab Foodie Brothers.

I drop the files back into the drawer. "There's nothing!" The frustration is like acid in my throat. "Maybe on the bookcase there's—"

The sound of laughter outside stops us. "Someone's

back! We need to get out of here," Ajay says, peeking under the door. "No one's in the kitchen, at least. They must be in the dining room. I think we can reach the exit."

I slide the drawer back into the desk. As I juggle my phone, its light catches on something in the corner. A whiteboard, like they have at school.

Ajay starts to turn the knob.

"Wait!" I whisper. I scramble over to the whiteboard and hold up my phone.

Samosa and empanada platter with sweet-and-sour sauce and assorted chutneys
Adobo masala dosa
Ube gulab jamun

I can barely breathe. These are exactly what was on the Banana Leaf menu the week of my spring break. I remember because I had to explain to a tourist that samosas and empanadas aren't just "meat Pop-Tarts," as he'd suggested.

Something clatters outside, and I don't have to see Ajay's face to know that he's sending me a *let's go!* glare.

I take a photo of the whiteboard. The camera flash fills the room; I could kick myself for such an attention-drawing action. But this is exactly the kind of evidence we need to start proving that the Darlingtons stole our recipes.

I stumble over to Ajay as he slowly tugs the door open. Whoever made the noise is gone, so we run for it. We make it halfway to the back door when we hear voices approaching.

Ajay yanks me behind an elephant statue just as the dining-area door swings open. "We ordered a golden elephant, not a bronze one." It's Gabriel, the Darlingtons' associate from the soft opening.

"You mean we have to get this back on the truck? It weighs a ton!" one of the movers says.

"The weight is not my problem. The color is. And if you don't get the correct statue in here by tomorrow, you'll be hearing from the Darlingtons' lawyers, got it?"

The mover grunts a yes, then adds, "But after lunch. Or are you going to get your lawyers to harass us about that too?"

"I advise you to watch your tone, sir. The Darlingtons take their businesses very seriously." The threat in Gabriel's voice sends a chill running down my spine. "Now, about the tapestries . . ."

The dining-area door swings open and closed again, and their voices fade just enough for Ajay and me to spring into action. We sprint for the door, passing a countertop now laden with sandwiches and fries. Ajay grabs a fry on our way out and shoves it in his pocket.

We don't stop running until we've cleared the alley and

rounded the corner. I lean back against the Gomezes' souvenir shop and plant my hands on my burning thighs.

"That was close, but I think I got something that could help prove they ate at our truck!" I fumble for my phone and scroll to the whiteboard photo. My legs almost collapse under me. The photo is a white blob with black edges.

"I don't understand, I—"

Ajay peers over my shoulder. "The flash must have bounced right back into the camera lens."

I can make out a few letters here and there, but there's no way someone like Tamra Wells would consider this hard evidence. "That was all for nothing, then."

Ajay wipes a bead of sweat off his forehead. I catch a glimpse of the french fry sticking out of his pocket.

"Why are you always stealing snacks?" Between that and the piecrust he took yesterday, his pockets must be filthy.

"I . . . um . . . I'm a growing boy?"

I snort. "We have a food truck. You can eat whenever you want."

"Yeah, but sometimes I—"

Squeak.

My stomach drops. "What. Was. That."

Ajay's eyes shift left to right, looking at anything but me. "What was what? I didn't hear anything?"

I force myself to standing and poke him in his bomber-jacketed chest. "I don't have to watch a ton of crime dramas to know when someone looks guilty. What was that noise?"

He wrings his empty hands. Then, to my horror, a gray, whiskered nose nudges out from his jacket pocket.

I don't realize I'm screaming until I'm out of breath. "You carry a *rat* around with you?"

"This is Whirligig. Whirl for short." I swear the rat waves at me with its whiskers.

"You *named* it?" My arms explode in goose bumps.

"He was getting lonely staying at home all day."

"You work at a food truck. *Our* food truck! The health inspector was just there!"

Ajay shakes his head, cutting off my line of thinking. "No one's seen him."

"Are you sure? Because if the health inspector ever caught that thing anywhere near the Banana Leaf, we'd be shut down in a second."

"That's why I keep him hidden. You think I'm wearing this huge jacket for fun? Yeah, it's stylish, but I have to wear three layers of deodorant in this heat."

I shake my head. "Too much, Ajay."

"What? The deodorant?"

"Everything!" I flail my arms in emphasis.

"Well, if you want my help, you're going to have to let my sidekick tag along too. That's part of the deal."

"You and these deals!" The universe had to make my new ally a rodent-toting, deodorant-slathered boy, didn't it? "Fine, fine. But promise you'll make sure no one sees it. And my donut scrunchie is back in the rotation."

Ajay's hand goes to his pocket to give Whirl a pat. I think I'm going to puke.

"Promise," he says. "Hey, did you know whirligig water beetles have two pairs of eyes? It lets them see above and below the water's surface at the same time. They'd be the best detectives. They'd get proof on the Darlingtons in no time."

"I—I can't handle your random facts right now. Why do—" I pause, a lightbulb flickering on in my brain. "Ripley: The nickname your family has for you. Like Ripley's Believe It or Not!"

His lips curve into a shy smile. "You know, you're one of the few people who's ever gotten that. Most people think it's because my parents like *Alien* or that movie where that guy steals someone's identity. But it's because my dad and I are huge trivia fans. His nickname for me just stuck."

"It all makes complete sense now. It's like you know a little bit about everything."

"I do," he says with a proud grin. "Believe it or not."

His joke brings a small laugh out of me, despite my gloom. "It's a good thing I've got you on my side, then." Because without any files or clear pictures of the Darlingtons' schemes, I've got nothing.

9

T'S BEEN THREE DAYS SINCE THE SOFT OPEN—
ing, two days since my salon confrontation with the
Darlingtons, and thirty minutes since Grandma rushed me
to get ready for tea with the Seashell Squad and the Coral
Beach Belles Women's Club this afternoon. I'd never seen
Grandma giddier than when I told her about this exclusive,
once-a-year high tea. Apparently, these teas are so popular
that people have to make reservations. Claire's mother, chair
of the Belles, set this up a whole month ago.

So today I have to put on a dress and go with Grandma
to hold teacups with our pinkies up and curtsy or whatever
it is people do at teas. I can't even wear my donut dress, after
my deal with Ajay. What I'd rather do is hang at the truck
with Dad, Mr. Ram, and Ajay and try to find a way to protect my family's business.

The Seashell Squad group chat has been flooded with talk about primping for an English-style afternoon tea at the fancy hotel by the water. It's saved me from more gushing over the Fab Foodie Brothers, but it's added extra pressure to dress and act just like the Seashells.

On my bed, I lay out my two options: taco dress and navy-blue skater dress. I send a picture of them to Catalina. If my sister were here for the summer like she was supposed to be, she'd be the one at afternoon tea with me today, not Grandma.

Mila: Which one? Tea with grandma + friends at the Trade Winds

Catalina: Ooh la la tea at Trade Winds? That's what the colonizers want you to do.

Catalina: Joke lang! Blue. You wear the taco dress too much.

Mila: Is there such a thing as wearing a taco dress too much?

Ten minutes and a drop of MettleMix later, I'm in the car with Grandma. My hair is combed and my face is washed. I even dug out a floral-print headband too.

I catch my reflection in the car's side window, and my mouth droops like runny icing on the whole look. This is me on my best behavior with Grandma, as Dad asked. I brush a crumb off the flowy skirt of the navy dress.

Grandma notices the movement. The woman sees everything. "If you need new clothes, we can go shopping after."

And spend the afternoon with her critiquing my "figure" and complaining that I don't dress girly enough?

"Thanks, but I'd like to get home and"—I reach for any excuse to hole myself up in my room—"read those books you got me." Grandma's a bookworm. She bought me a whole Chronicles of Narnia set and assigned it as summer reading (I guess she has that authority?), so she would understand the need for some uninterrupted time.

Grandma hmphs. "You only ever wear that dress or those childish food ones. Your father should be spending more time raising you to be a proper young lady than on that nonsense truck of his."

I flinch as if she's pinched me. "It's not nonsense, it's his dream."

Her laugh is bitter. "He has two children to take care of. He doesn't have time for silly dreams. And with that new restaurant in town?"

"What have you heard?" I admittedly don't have an ear in the Coral Beach senior citizen community. But customers are customers. I want to know what people think.

"That they're serving the same food as the Banana Leaf. I told him the restaurant business is hard, that his food isn't special enough. I knew from the beginning that he and Ram were going to fail."

That feels like a punch to the gut. Dad's food is fantastic.

And let's not forget—ever—that some of those fusion dishes, like the turon lassi, were my ideas. Other than my snooping around the Darlingtons, Dad's been supportive of everything I've done. He bought me new sneakers when I tried (and failed) to get on the basketball team at my old school. He stood in a long line with me to get a movie poster signed by my favorite actress. And he even printed out the time conversion schedule between here and the Philippines so I never miscalculated Mom's call times.

I can't imagine how tough it is for Dad to deal with Grandma's never-ending doubts. Maybe that's why he's so great to me. Finding a way to shut down Marigold and Myth would be the perfect way to pay him back.

"Dad's truck isn't going to fail," I say. "The Darlingtons may have an identical menu, but Dad's food is way better. Ideas are one thing. But with cooking, it's all in the execution."

Grandma pulls into a parking spot, then turns to me. "Your grandpa and I didn't come to this country and pay for his engineering schooling so he can serve snacks out of a truck."

She shakes her head. Her heavily hair-sprayed bob barely moves. "This was not our American dream. Where's his stable job? The savings he should have by now? He's supposed to live in his own home and be providing for you all."

Grandma's wrong. He's doing just fine at providing for

our family, especially since I required some shifting around of their family plan. I'm six years younger than Catalina because my parents weren't sure they could have another child. When I was born healthy, Mom called me her *milagro*, "miracle" in Tagalog. That's why my name is Mila.

Grandma's just in a mean mood, and she needs to know I don't share her opinion. "He's a good dad. And this is *his* dream."

She shuts off the engine and opens her door. "Yes, I suppose I should accept that his dream isn't the one your grandfather and I had for him. But like you said, it's all in the execution, isn't it? You should open your eyes, read those bills at home that your dad hasn't been opening. Then you'll see how pursuing this dream is really going."

She spits out that last phrase like it's a bone shard in a meatball, and her tone makes my stomach curdle. She knows something I don't. Dad, Mom, and Mr. Ram shield me from a lot of the money stuff. Should I have been paying more attention?

Grandma grabs her purse and shuts the door. For a moment, I'm alone in her car. Is the ringing in my ears from anger at Grandma for being so rough on Dad? Or is this me starting to realize that the Banana Leaf may not be as successful as I thought?

I can't ask her about it. Even if she were willing to share, she'd probably say it in the most negative way possible. Then she'd dig into why I asked.

A sudden sadness washes over me. It seems like I'm forced to hide *more* of myself these days, trying harder to fit in to please others. It's exhausting.

A tap on the window makes me jump. Grandma's lips are pursed and she's reapplying her signature red lipstick in the side mirror. "Hurry up, Mila."

The hostess shows us to our tables, where the Seashells and their mothers have left two seats open for Grandma and me. As we squeeze in, I scan the dining room for clues as to what to do. No curtsying: good. But cloth napkins? I copy Lane and drape the napkin over my lap.

"So glad you could join us, Mrs. Pascual!" says Mrs. Armstrong, Lane's mother. Her teeth are as spotless white as the napkins, her wavy dark red hair equally flawless. She turns her hazel eyes on me. "I take it your mother is still in . . . um, where again?"

"The Philippines," Grandma replies for me.

"Right, lovely," Mrs. Armstrong says. "Lane's old nanny was from the Philippines."

I catch myself before I do my awkward wide-eyed look. I'm here to show how well I fit in. It doesn't help when folks bring up their nannies or nurses every time I mention that I'm Filipino.

It actually makes me glad that Catalina isn't here after all. I can imagine exactly how that conversation would go.

"And where is your family from?" my sister would ask.

Mrs. Armstrong would smile. "Oh, you know, all over the place in Europe."

Then Catalina would pick up her teacup ever so daintily. "Ah, Europe. Our old colonizers were from Europe." She'd sip, then smile. "Have you heard of Magellan?"

While I'm busy missing my sister, conversation has moved on to the hot topic of the day, week, month, maybe even year: Chip and Chaz Darlington.

I stay quiet, but at some point, I worry it's too obvious I'm not saying a word. With the adults wrapped up in themselves, I try to steer the conversation with my friends toward anything else. *How's ballet, Karina and Elle? Is that a new haircut, Claire? Lane, how's your dog?*

My distractions only last a minute before someone invariably mentions what they saw Chip order at Starbucks, what glamorous celebrity made a guest appearance on Chaz's TikTok, whether the brothers are still secretly in town and hiding among us.

Before I can stop myself, I snort aloud.

Karina raises an eyebrow. "What's so funny?"

"The thought of them hiding among us. Like aliens or spies or something."

Claire rolls her eyes. "I didn't mean it *that* way, Mila. I meant like how celebrities wear hats or fake glasses so we don't know they're sitting next to us at the movies."

My face must pinch at the idea, because across from me, Lane's eyebrows scrunch. "What, do you have a problem with the Fab Foodie Brothers? Weren't you at their soft opening? They barely showed any of the cool stuff, with all those commercial breaks they took."

Suddenly, I feel everyone's eyes on me. Good thing I had that MettleMix. This is my chance to make them understand, to get them on my side. "I did go to their soft opening. But their food is just like ours at the Banana Leaf. That's fishy, don't you think?"

Elle says "Definitely" at the same time Karina says "No." My stomach flips.

"My parents said that Marigold and Myth is just what this town needs," Karina continues. "Not as many people are visiting Coral Beach these days. Even the cruise ships are starting to pass us by. We need this. Coral Beach needs this."

The tension in our conversation practically bubbles over.

Claire shrugs. "I haven't tried the Darlingtons' food, so I don't know."

"Me neither," says Lane.

"What did you think, Elle?" Karina asks. She knows better than to weigh in herself, considering she hasn't tasted the Banana Leaf's fare.

I see the battle happening behind Elle's eyes. She agrees with me, but she might not want to alienate her friends. Her mouth curves into a nervous smile. "Well, there's room in Coral Beach for both Marigold and Myth and the Banana Leaf, right?"

Finding myself alone again hurts just as much as I thought it would. "Yeah. I guess."

"Hey, what happened to your bracelet, Mila?" Karina asks.

It's only then that I realize my pink friendship bracelet is missing. I can't remember the last time I had it, either. "I—I don't know. I might've lost it."

"Oh, I lose mine all the time! Once it got caught on the toilet handle," Claire giggles.

"I'll keep looking for it," I say. "But we can always make a new one, right?"

The pause before Karina says yes drives her point home: I'm still their friend. Sort of.

"Making new bracelets might be a fun thing to do at your birthday party, right, Lane?" Elle pipes up. She turns to me. "Lane's dad has this amazing yacht, and at the end

96

of summer, he always hires a professional chef and an arts teacher and we—ow!"

Elle jumps, then snaps her mouth shut. I can't tell who kicked her under the table, but I wait for one of the other Seashells to finish her story. When no one does, I get the message loud and clear: I'm not invited.

I take a sip of tea to hide my face with the cup. It stings, not being included. Thankfully a server comes by to clear our empty plates, and the awkward silence is filled with the clink of tableware.

Then Elle tries to shift everyone's focus to a new, non-Darlingtons topic. Even with her help, it doesn't work. Eventually, talk circles back to the Fab Foodie Brothers. This time, I know better. I smile and laugh with the rest of them, and no one mentions my missing bracelet again.

I wipe my palms on my napkin. I wish I'd brought the MettleMix with me. Maybe an extra boost of magical courage could've helped turn around this mess of a conversation. Maybe some other blend of herbs and incantations would've made them listen to me.

But I know that none of Catalina's potions would've helped in that way. She's adamant about only using her skills for good, which means amplifying positive things like calmness and contentment. I could dump all her herbal blends into this flower-painted teapot, and my friends might get a temporary mood lift, but I'd still be grumpy. (And we'd all probably be nauseous.)

I sip my tea. Now that I think about it, making people dislike the Darlingtons *would* be using albularyo skills for good. Maybe I can get Catalina to see it that way too.

I set down my teacup, slump back in my chair, and catch a few snippets of conversation at the tables around us. The adults are talking about the good the new restaurant will do for the local economy. From a nearby table, I hear a few awed whispers about Marigold and Myth and how someone's hoping to make reservations for opening week. It all makes the scones taste like ash, the black currant jam like tar.

Then I realize no one else is sitting as sloppily as I am. Grandma shoots a glare at me—again, that woman sees everything. I pop up and straighten my back. When Lane says something about her Maltese wagging his butt, I smile . . . until she says he does it when he hears the Fab Foodie Brothers' theme song.

I shovel down the rest of my scone and burn my mouth on hot tea just so I can get out of Trade Winds faster.

10

EVERYTHING SEEMS TO GO WRONG DURING Monday's lunch rush. First, I forget my potions at home because Dad hurries me out the door. Then throughout the day, things burn and spill, customers frown, the tip jar sits nearly empty. We don't finish cleaning up the truck until almost four in the afternoon.

The ride home is quiet. I check my texts, but nothing from my LA friends yet. This time last year at camp, we were planning our group project: a three-tier jungle-themed cake. Yes, phones were off-limits, but we barely even noticed. Today, I grip my phone like I can squeeze more interaction from it. Oddly enough, it works!

Mom: Hi from the Philippines! Your grandpa's doing much better. I even caught him trying to sneak out for karaoke with his friends.

The text message includes a picture of mom, smiling wide and makeup-free, her long black hair pulled up in a ponytail. Next to her is Grandpa Ben, pretending to look grumpy, but the twinkle in his eye gives away the fact that he's happy Mom's there.

Dad's voice cuts in. "You're smiling."

"A text from Mom," I say, angling the phone to him while we idle at a red light.

"Your grandpa looks like he's back to his cranky old self. That means Mom might be home soon."

I catch the hope in his voice: he misses her as much as I do. Maybe we're both a little lonely here in Coral Beach. But Dad has Mr. Ram, while I'm still not sure where I stand with the Seashells, especially after butting heads with them about their chef idols. "I hope so."

Dad drops me off before spending a few late hours at his renewable energy job. I feel like I've failed at helping today, even though I did everything I could.

After unloading groceries for Grandma, I change into knee-length shorts and a taco-print shirt (I own many food-themed things. Ajay can't ban all of them) and settle in front of my computer.

My phone rings, but I don't recognize the number. "Hello?"

"Hey, it's Ajay. My uncle gave me your number. I would've

just texted but he went into this whole etiquette rant."

"Oh." I try to wipe away the disappointment that it isn't Mom, but it leaves me feeling icky anyway.

"You okay?"

I put my phone on speaker so I can open my laptop. "Yeah. Still exhausted from that lunch rush. Thanks for helping me clean up the spilled fish sauce."

Unfortunately, nothing in my potions bag can help my tiredness. Ages ago, I asked Catalina for some sort of energy-boosting potion to help me stay awake in Mr. Toleno's ultra-boring science class. She laughed about how there is such a thing—coffee—and that because I was too young to drink tons of it, I'd have to slog through snore-inducing classes just like she did.

Siblings: they're helpful until they're not.

"No problem. But it wasn't all bad. Remember that customer with the Great Dane as tall as I am? Did you know dogs' mouths aren't cleaner than humans' mouths? It's a common—"

"Ajay, focus. What'd you call for?"

"Oh, right. What's your email address? I need to send you some research I did on the Darlingtons."

Now *this* is the kind of surprise I enjoy. Having Ajay doing extra research while I'm tied up is fantastic.

It occurs to me then that some kids would be self-conscious

being excited about things like research and school. But Ajay seems confident in who he is and eager to share that with others. I'm a little jealous of him for that. I'd have to know who I was first to be that confident.

I give him my email address, and he clacks away at a keyboard. "In the meantime, I want you to do an online search for the Darlingtons."

I roll my eyes. "You think I haven't?"

"Trust me, do it again."

As I type their names into the search bar, there's a clear squeak through the phone, and I shudder.

"Whirligig says hi, Mila."

"Nope. I am not saying hello to a rat."

"Rude."

All the usual results come up when I hit Search. Their shows, restaurants, interviews, talk show appearances. "What am I supposed to be seeing?"

"You know how to narrow results by date range? Look for anything before Chip Darlington graduated culinary school."

I type "Chip and Chaz Darlington" into the search bar, tell it to find anything older than 2015, then hit Enter.

"Huh," I say.

"Tell me what you see."

"I see"—I scroll down the page—"nothing. Every listing is about some other Darlington. None of the pictures even look like Chip or Chaz." No social media accounts, no old school pictures, not even any high school sports records.

Something feels off, like a pan that won't sit flat on the stove. Dad ran varsity track over a decade ago, and all those results still come up. Even searching for my name yields some results, like when Carlos, Molly, and I got featured in our school paper about Kids Baking Camp.

"Exactly," Ajay says. "They're my mom's age, so it's not like they were born in the Dark Ages, before internet."

I reach for any explanation. They grew up in the middle of nowhere? No, their website says they grew up in Los Angeles. So what gives?

"It's like they appeared out of nowhere," I say.

"Right, and that's not the weirdest or worst of it. Check your email."

An article from 2016 pops up when I click the link in Ajay's email. It's a restaurant review from the *San Mariano Gazette*. San Mariano sits right between here and Los Angeles. Dad and I stopped there for gas and a slice of prosciutto-topped pizza on our way up here.

"New in Town: BarbeCool." The article mentions that

two brothers started a restaurant that fused all-you-can-eat Korean barbecue and burritos. People could grill the meats they wanted, then choose their banchan, and roll it up in a fresh tortilla. The article was updated a year later to state that the restaurant had been sold. There are no pictures of any of the restaurant owners.

"A fusion restaurant," I say. "The concept sounds pretty cool. What are these other links?"

I click, and a plain, outdated website comes up. Another Korean barbecue burrito place in San Mariano, but not BarbeCool. Prime BBBQ (the extra B is for "burrito"), the website says. My heart flops around as my brain struggles to catch up.

"Huh. So that first article is about a hot new fusion restaurant," I begin, struggling to piece together the new information, "created by some unnamed brothers, in the same town where—according to this website—another small business was already killing it at the same exact thing."

My mouth goes dry.

"This is exactly what the Fab Foodie Brothers are doing in Coral Beach!" I blurt. "But how can we be sure it's—"

The sound of a phone ringing cuts me short. I curse internally at Ajay for not even giving me a heads-up that he's about to add someone else to our call.

"Hello, Prime BBBQ!" a voice says. She sounds young, like a high schooler manning the takeout orders.

"Hi, this is the San Mariano location, right?" Ajay asks.

"Yes, it is," the girl responds. "Are you making a reservation, or would you like a pickup or delivery order?"

"Neither. We want to ask you about BarbeCool."

The line goes so quiet I think the call has dropped.

"Hello?" I finally croak.

"We are the *original* all-you-can-eat Korean barbecue and burritos restaurant here," the girl responds. She forces the words out like every syllable is a pulled tooth. "If you want food by those two know-nothing frauds, you'll have to go somewhere else."

"Two frauds? You mean the Darlingtons? Are they the ones who opened BarbeCool?"

More silence, and I can practically envision the gears turning in Ajay's head at all this.

"Like I said, you'll have to go somewhere else," the girl says, her tone hard. "I'm not allowed to talk about them. The lawyers, they . . . Anyway, if you're not going to order anything, goodbye."

Then the Prime BBBQ line drops and it's just Ajay and me again.

"Did you hear how angry she was when you mentioned

the Darlingtons?" Ajay says. "The BarbeCool owners—it's got to be them!"

"I agree. They must've had something to do with this competing restaurant, or this person wouldn't have gotten so upset." I scoot to the edge of my chair. "What if this is a pattern for the Darlingtons? They find a concept that's super popular, replicate it where they know there's a guaranteed customer base, then bankrupt the little guy."

My hands shake as I spout out my theory. Not only is it possible the Darlingtons might not be who they say they are, they might have a long, secret history of stealing from small businesses too. And we're up next.

"We need to talk to these Prime BBBQ folks right away," Ajay says. And of course, he fails to alert me again that he's trying to call the restaurant on this same line. But this time, it rings and rings, with no answer.

"I don't think they're going to answer our calls anymore," I say. Tamra Wells's warning about proof flits into my head. "So maybe we should check out this Prime BBBQ place in person and talk to the owners," I add. "We can see if the food matches the BarbeCool menu too."

"Good idea. You think your dad or grandma will take us? My parents are veg, and Ram Uncle hates driving, which is weird for a food truck owner."

The idea of spending more time in the car with Grandma

sounds like a nightmare, but Dad? I have just the ticket to a mini road trip and dinner out.

"Lucky for us, someone's got a birthday coming up."

And my birthday wish, when I blow out those candles, will be to drive the Darlingtons out of Coral Beach for good.

11

AFTER AJAY HANGS UP, I FACETIME MY SIS-
ter. She's become more involved in her college Filipino folk dance troupe, and the last three times I've called, she's been at practice.

As if the universe knows I need a win, Catalina answers.

"Hey, Mila!" She smiles wide, revealing that familiar gap between her front teeth. Her wavy hair cascades around her shoulders. She and Mom have always kept their hair long, while my haircuts tend to mimic Dad's. Why spend time styling in the bathroom when you could be chopping and sizzling in the kitchen?

But seeing her face makes all those differences insignificant. I didn't realize how much I've missed her.

When we first moved here, I called Catalina two or three times a week. With her starting college months six before, I figured she'd understand how fish-out-of-water I felt. It soon became clear that she didn't face the same friend-making challenges. Her interests—dance, non-food-print clothing, and folk healing—led to her collaborating with new people all the time. But cooking has never been an activity I share with many outside my family, Carlos, Molly, and Kids Baking Camp. That whole saying about too many cooks spoiling the broth? Totally true. And it doesn't help that Coral Beach tastes tend to skew as safe as vanilla ice cream.

So Catalina simply didn't relate to what I was going through. It became easier for us to talk about the truck and classes, rather than how much I missed her, Mom, and our old home. Then her dance troupe started ramping up practice, and now it seems like we don't even talk at all some weeks.

Catalina's cheery greeting still feels like a warm, familiar hug. String lights hang on the wall behind her, shining on the torn-out fashion magazine spreads taped underneath. It's almost like I'm sitting in her room with her, like old times. Almost.

"How's it going?" she asks. "How's Coral Beach?"

"The same. Working at the truck, dodging Grandma. But I did sign up for a weekend jazz dance intensive in August." It's not traditional Filipino dance, but it's artsy and a way to hang out with the Seashell Squad. I'd think Catalina would appreciate that. Grandma loved the idea and even paid for it.

Catalina raises an eyebrow. "Afternoon tea at the Trade Winds *and* a jazz dance class? You're like a whole new person! How about the Fab Foodie Brothers? Any more celebrity sightings?"

"That's why I'm calling." I cough to clear my throat. "Hear me out: I think the Darlingtons stole Dad's recipes, and I think they've done something like this before." I explain what Ajay and I have uncovered so far.

Catalina's thick eyebrows scrunch together. "That's terrible! What did Dad say?"

I explain Dad's less-than-enthusiastic response, and she nods. "Figures. Dad may be a firecracker in the kitchen, but all Grandma's talk about being a polite model citizen gets to him. Remember when he *thanked* that police officer for giving him a parking ticket?"

I chuckle at the memory. We had a family day at Huntington Beach, complete with multiple layers of coconut-scented sunscreen and rapidly melting ice cream sundaes in waffle cones. By the time we got back to the car, the parking meter was flashing its red EXPIRED. A grim-faced officer stood next to it. Dad tried, for a minute, to negotiate his way out of it before taking the ticket with a grumbled "Thanks, I guess." For weeks after, Catalina and I thanks-I-guessed each other every time one of us annoyed the other.

"Dad hates ruffling feathers. We've got to help him," Catalina says. "Do you need me to mobilize my TikTok followers?"

I snort. "You have like, forty followers, and half of those are family."

She glares at me. "Well, do you want my help or not?"

"Yes, but you can tell your follower army to stand down." I pause to make sure Grandma's not buzzing around outside my door. "Your albularyo training, all that witchy stuff—do you have anything that could help us prove the Darlingtons stole the recipes?"

She crosses her arms and leans toward the camera. "First, it's not just 'witchy stuff.' I'm exploring the folklore and magic of our Filipino roots, like you should be doing. But you don't speak a word of Ilocano or Tagalog, you don't call me 'manang' or 'ate,' and you didn't even show interest in Filipino food until non-Filipinos started gushing about Dad's truck."

In typical Catalina fashion, she doesn't pull her punches. Her words sting. She was born here, like I was, but she's made a big effort to try to reconnect with our family's heritage. She had Mom guiding her through it—I suppose they had to fill those hour-long car rides to Catalina's dance performances somehow. I, on the other hand, barely poke at the dirt that sits on top of those roots. It's intimidating to dig deeper when I'm already this bad and bungling at the little I know.

Fitting in here in Coral Beach, with its eerie sameness, is hard enough. The same type of quirky for each gift shop, the same type of dull beach-tan paint slapped on anything that could be construed as too different. We don't even have school uniforms, yet everyone seems to wear the same kinds of clothes to school, down to the same brand.

Catalina wouldn't know how hard it is. We lived in a diverse suburb of LA our whole lives, up until she moved into her equally diverse college dorm and I came up here. I bet she's never walked into a cafeteria where she could count the number of faces like hers on one hand.

But somehow, she considers me less Filipino because I've never gotten my foot trapped between tinikling poles or tried balut, because my tongue has trouble with the language from a place an ocean away. And some people consider me less American because I eat rice for breakfast and my skin's naturally a shade darker than theirs.

Running between two worlds feels impossible when the goalposts keep moving.

"I didn't call to get picked on, Catalina. I'm asking for

your help. And inviting you to my birthday party in San Mariano on Saturday."

"Sorry, Mila. I didn't mean to get so defensive. But come on, 'witchy stuff'? I don't call your interests 'overpriced, snooty belly stuff,'" she says. I can't help but laugh at what she thinks being a foodie is.

"I take back what I said. Your potions are amazing. Your Rage Cage single-handedly kept me from exploding when Grandma deleted the *Top Chef* season finale I recorded."

The smile returns to her face. "I should be able to make it to San Mariano, if I can borrow my roommate's car. And as for that 'witchy stuff,' I have a book."

She flits off-screen, then reappears with a bright blue paperback. "There might be a spell or potion in here that can help. Like a truth serum."

I nod. "That's exactly what I'm looking for. If I can get the Marigold and Myth staff to take it, maybe I can get to the bottom of this recipe theft."

I lean closer to my screen, as if I can read over Catalina's shoulder.

"There's something in here about a ritual involving trapping a fly in a bottle. It kinda works like a voodoo doll. You can put the bottled fly in cold water to make the person cold, or put it on the stove to roast them."

I gag at the image. "Catalina, I don't want to torture the Darlingtons. Or a poor fly, for that matter. Can you find something a little less gruesome?"

"Just giving you options, sis." Catalina's nose wrinkles as she continues to flip through her book. "This doesn't have many actual potion recipes in it. I can't believe I spent my latte money on this."

My shoulders sag. I need to find a way to get the Darlingtons to confess. My snooping and questioning haven't worked, and we have less than two weeks to prove the theft.

"Wait!" Catalina jumps up. Whatever she's resting her phone on moves, and I find myself looking at the ceiling. "There's mention of gayuma, love potions! I bet I can do some research online and tweak it, and we can make it ourselves. Like an anti-love potion."

The gears in my brain turn. "An anti-love potion, like something that gets people to hate each other? If I get the Marigold and Myth staff to start bickering, they might turn on one another and confess the whole thing."

Catalina nods quickly. "Just like on those court shows that Mom loves!"

"Right. This might work. But make it ourselves? No way I can do that."

My sister frowns. "You know, a surefire way to fail at

something is to not believe you can do it."

I scrunch my nose. "What's that supposed to mean?"

"It means that brewing potions is one thing, but actually believing in the magic with your whole heart and soul? That's a big part of what makes it work."

"Easy for you to say. The potions actually work when you make them."

She sighs, and so do I. We've had this conversation before, and we always seem to miss each other's point.

"Anyway," I say, "I don't know if we should be mixing potions based on some online discussion board chatter. I want the truth, but I don't want to poison people."

She crosses her arms. "You know, to get the job done, you're going to have to get your hands dirty."

"No, Catalina! We run a food truck. In what world do you think I'd want to poison anyone?"

She casually waves a hand like she didn't just suggest I trick people into ingesting something toxic. "Fine, fine. I can ask around the albularyo community here for help. You remember Jeanie, the owner of the bookstore I took you to on family weekend? She's also an albularyo and is studying a few other folk healing arts. I've been working at the bookstore counter in exchange for lessons and harder-to-find ingredients. She might be able to help. But I'm warning you, her services on a custom potion like this aren't going to be easy . . . or cheap."

I'll take any help I can get. "How much do you think it'll cost?"

"Keep your tip money, Mila. I owe my little sister a birthday gift."

12

SPENDING MY THIRTEENTH BIRTHDAY SEE—
ing my sister, filling up on Korean barbecue burritos,
and digging up dirt on the Darlingtons? This is going to be
great. I wear my best non-taco shirt for the occasion. It even
has lace around the collar.

One of the B's in the red-lit Prime BBBQ sign is burned
out, and Dad drives past twice before we finally see the place.

Ajay, Grandma, and I share the cramped back seat.
I'm stuck in the middle, my shins freezing from the air-
conditioning vent aimed straight at them. Grandma fell
asleep almost as soon as we got in the car. A few sharp turns
resulted in her elbow wedged uncomfortably against my ribs.

Ajay's thankfully left his bomber jacket—and Whirligig—
at home. The rat is used to a few hours alone on the weekend,
he explained. It's a full day at the food truck that kicks

separation anxiety into high gear. I pretended to understand what he was talking about. But mostly, I wanted to stop discussing rodent psychology right before my birthday dinner.

Only a handful of other cars sit in the parking lot, and they're gathered in front of the laundromat at the other end of the plaza.

Dad shuts off the car. "You sure this is it? It looks a little dead."

It's exactly how I expected Prime BBBQ to look. Especially since I suspect the Darlingtons stole their thunder and left town with the profits.

Grandma wakes up and yawns at the nearly empty parking lot. "We could have just had lunch at the Trade Winds instead of driving out here."

"Well, it *is* a little early in the day," Mr. Ram says, unbuckling his seat belt. "Maybe the dinner crowd comes later?"

Across the lot, a car empties. One of the figures waves.

"It's Catalina!" I say. Once Ajay gets up and out of the way, I sprint toward my sister, wrapping her in a hug. She's in a cream-colored knit crop top that I'd never wear and that Mom would probably shake her head at. At the thought of Mom, I squeeze my sister tighter.

After I step back, she tugs over her friend, a tall Latinx

person with a lightning-bolt-shaped nose stud. "This is Avery," Catalina says. "Their pronouns are they and them."

Avery offers me a fist bump. "Happy birthday, Mila." Then they notice Grandma staring. "Catalina, you didn't tell me you have *another* sister!"

Grandma literally giggles before introducing herself, then Dad and Mr. Ram say hello as well. Ajay waves, then tries to wow everyone with some statistics about lightning-strike probability.

We enter Prime BBBQ, and I approach the reservations podium. "Party of seven for Mila?"

The hostess, a Korean woman closer to Grandma's age, offers me a welcoming smile. A window that opens into the kitchen reveals an older man, also closer to Grandma's age, on his phone. In the corner of the dining room are a teenage girl and a young boy, sharing earbuds and an iPad. I assume these are the hostess's grandkids, and I wonder if the girl is the one who answered the phone when Ajay and I called the other day. The restaurant is otherwise empty.

"We have two tables set up for you, right next to each other. Follow me," the hostess says.

We walk by a few framed articles on the wall.

Top 10 Restaurants in San Mariano—2013, 2014, 2015.

That other Korean barbecue burrito place, BarbeCool, opened in 2016, ending Prime's streak.

We arrange ourselves around the tables, the adults at one, the younger generation at the other. Knowing Dad, he'll want to man both tables, which is fine with me. He's the pro.

The hostess lights the grills set into the tables. By the time she returns a few minutes later with a tray full of banchan, warmth radiates off the grills and onto our drooling faces.

"I haven't had kimchi this good since we were back in LA," Mr. Ram says. He closes his eyes as he eats.

"I don't think I've had kimchi at all since moving to Coral Beach," I add. The disappointment must be clear in my voice because Dad's smile droops a little.

Avery asks Dad polite questions about work—engineering work, not the food truck—and Dad, Grandma, and Mr. Ram get dragged into an uninteresting, not-about-food conversation.

Something bumps my forearm. A small box, wrapped in gold polka-dot paper. "Happy birthday," Catalina says with a wink.

My pulse jumps. "Is this the anti-love potion?" I whisper.

"Sort of. Jeanie didn't approve of the idea of a hate potion. She said it's not in the spirit of what she does as an albularyo. So we compromised and made it an 'extremely annoyed' potion instead. It only lasts two or three minutes after the person ingests it. It's the best I could do."

A wrench in my plan. Hatred would probably make people

confess to major crimes like they do in Mom's court dramas, but extreme annoyance might mean someone just goes quiet and sits off by themselves. Even when I'm extremely annoyed at Grandma—which is most of the time—I don't yell at her.

It will have to do. Time is running out before the grand opening of Marigold and Myth.

"So the potion just makes the person annoyed? Vexed?" Ajay mutters to himself. "Like a vex hex?"

Catalina's nose crinkles. "Well, technically, it's not a hex. It's a potion—"

Ajay rolls his eyes. "We're not calling it the 'extreme annoyance potion' every single time, are we?"

I bite back a laugh. "He's got a point. Inaccurate as the nickname may be, I'm willing to try this VexHex witchy stuff."

Catalina shakes her head. "I swear, sometimes I think you *try* to get on my nerves."

I see Grandma eyeing the box, so I give it a shake like I'm trying to guess my present. I expect to hear a bottle clinking around, but it's muffled by something. "Thanks! I wonder what's in here."

"Don't get too excited," Catalina says. "We bought you socks."

Avery pops out of their engineering conversation. "Correction. They're not just socks. They're taco-print socks."

Catalina unwraps her chopsticks. "To match that dress of yours."

Ajay groans. I'm hit with such a pang from missing my sister that I feel it right in my gut. Or it could be hunger, because just then, Dad lays thick strips of pork belly across the grill.

Ajay takes advantage of the loud sizzle to lean over. "How are we supposed to question the hostess with Dad and Ram Uncle right here?"

My smile turns mischievous. "That's where Catalina and Avery come in."

Catalina and I laid out a whole plan the other night. It hinges on Avery challenging Dad and Mr. Ram to a good old-fashioned eating contest. They're never ones to back down from competitive eating, and Avery was more than happy to score a free meal in exchange for giving Catalina a ride.

"So when do we start?" Catalina asks.

"When the pork belly's almost cooked. Dad will be too busy with both grills to see Ajay and I sneak away." And the process of racing to eat mass quantities of meat will take care of the rest.

I nibble at a hot tortilla as I watch the pork belly brown. Acid bubbles in my throat. Not from the tortilla, but from the fact that we have to resort to all this to save the Banana

Leaf. If only Dad and Mr. Ram could understand what we're doing, if only they were on our side, we wouldn't have to make up these elaborate excuses.

A young white couple walks in and gets seated a few tables away. At least there's some business on a Saturday night.

I glance back at the pork belly, then meet Avery's gaze. *Now,* I mouth.

On cue, a smirk spreads across Avery's face. "You know, Mr. Pascual, I once stayed so long at an all-you-can-eat place that they asked me to leave so the staff could lock up and go home."

Dad takes the bait and laughs. "Well, I have my picture up at the Pho Hut for finishing their Supreme Bowl—two pounds of meat and noodles and a half gallon of broth—in record time."

Mr. Ram waves him off. "*Psh,* anyone can eat a lot of food. But you're in the presence of the winner of the melt-your-face spice-off at Thai Garden!"

Avery, Dad, and Mr. Ram erupt in a back-and-forth of one-upmanship, and before we know it, the eat-as-much-as-you-can challenge has morphed into eat-as-much-as-you-can-and-make-it-spicy!

Their digestive systems are not going to be kind to them tomorrow. But tonight, these three are raring to start. Dad waves over our hostess, and Avery strategically holds up a menu so that Dad and Mr. Ram don't see Ajay and I rise from our seats.

"Oh, clumsy me! I dropped kimchi on our shoes. Let's clean up!" I yank Ajay toward the back of the restaurant.

With Dad, Mr. Ram, and Avery arguing with Grandma and the hostess about how much meat is too much for one round—Avery keeps repeating "The limit does not exist!"— we head for the kitchen to speak to the chefs. Ajay's about to walk in when I grab his arm. The older man we'd seen on the phone earlier is in the kitchen all by himself. There are no other chefs.

"I hadn't realized only one person would be manning the kitchen right now," I say. "He's working on the other customers' orders. We can't bug him."

Ajay peers back at our table. The hostess is furiously scrawling down our table's orders. "We can't talk to her either."

I run a hand through my short hair. "We can't leave empty-handed. Who is going to give us the inside scoop on the Darlingtons?"

An odd stillness catches my attention. Like when there's a fountain running and you notice exactly when the water stops. I turn my head to see the teenage girl with the iPad eyeing me. She has straight black hair in a high ponytail, and the boy—who I'm not sure is even blinking as he watches the screen—looks a few years younger than me.

"The Darlingtons? If you're fans of *theirs*, you should leave right now," the girl says. Her brown eyes narrow.

I approach their table. Her tone tells me there's history, which is both promising and depressing.

"It's you—you're the one who answered the phone! Don't worry, we're not fans of theirs," I assure her.

It occurs to me then that this may be the first time I've ever said out loud that I don't love the Darlingtons. All this time, I think a part of me was hoping I was wrong, that I could brush it all aside as a mistake and go back to gushing about them with the Seashell Squad. That wouldn't save the truck and my family, though.

I clear my throat. "In fact, we think the Darlingtons are stealing ideas and recipes from other chefs."

The girl pulls out her earbuds and pushes the iPad in front of the little boy. He leans in, hogging the screen to himself. "How do I know I can trust you? You might be sent by their legal goons."

"Goons?" I blink. "Why would I—"

"Here," Ajay says. He has the Banana Leaf's Instagram account open and is showing the girl a month-old picture of me holding a turon lassi in front of our truck. "See? Small business. Fusion, like yours. We're on your side."

The girl lifts her chin, reading the caption and considering us.

I wish there was a way to make her consider faster. I don't want to risk Dad noticing our absence while they're waiting for the meat to cook. Also, the food smells delicious, and my stomach is begging me to return to my seat.

Finally, she purses her lips and motions us closer. "I'm Annie. Prime BBBQ belongs to my parents, but it's pretty much my grandparents running it now, and yeah, I help with the phones. My parents had to go back to work to pay off some business debts. They don't get here until later."

I gulp. "So how are the Darlingtons involved? Did they steal your parents' ideas too?"

Annie nods. "Almost the same exact menu. They just added some toasted sesame seeds and cilantro on top of stuff and said it was different. It was insulting."

I snort. "They changed the shape of the lumpia wrapper in our turon lassi. It's a triangle, instead of a fried-up roll that can double as a temporary straw. Pathetic."

Annie peers over my shoulder to check on her grandmother, the hostess. "What was worse is that they bullied our family. My uncle is a lawyer up in the Bay, so my dad threatened to sue them. The next day some guys in expensive suits showed up here at Prime."

My mouth goes dry despite the delicious smells around

me. I dread where Annie's story is headed.

"This was before they were popular, before they got their big TV break. I was younger than my brother then," she says, glancing at the iPad-entranced boy next to her. "But I remember that the suit guys looked mean and they handed Dad a thick manila envelope. He told us it was just some paperwork from the city, but I'm pretty sure it was legal stuff from the Darlingtons. Then my parents stopped talking about the Darlingtons at all. They even change the channel when there's a commercial of them."

No wonder she was wary we'd be tied to the Darlingtons. They stole her family's business, then threatened them into silence. A chill runs down my spine. Catalina's comment the other day flows back to me. *To get the job done, you're going to have to get your hands dirty.* The Darlingtons' hands sound filthy.

"What should I do, Annie? Report them to some business bureau? The police?" I hate that everyone else might have been right: this might be too much for a couple of kids to handle.

Annie sighs. "Think about it: you really believe those government types are going to side with some nobody Asian folks over the glamorous foodie Captain Americas? They didn't in San Mariano."

But Grandma works for the city government in Coral

Beach. She fits in, speaks English with only the tiniest accent, and sips overpriced tea at the Trade Winds. Coral Beach can't be like that, can it? "It's different," I say, uncertain.

I think of Catalina's colonization comments about Grandma and me. Do I have to be exactly like Grandma, like everyone else in Coral Beach, in order to feel like I belong? Must we mold ourselves to fit into spaces not necessarily made for us? Speak without accents, dine at the fancy tourist hotel, ignore when someone mocks us with a made-up Asian-sounding language. Even if we do everything we can to blend in, how do we know folks won't turn on us when we try to protect the spaces we've earned? Being an award-winning community-favorite restaurant didn't save Prime BBBQ. What if we and the Banana Leaf and our new home aren't any different?

The thought leaves a bitter taste.

"You know your town better, I guess. But I hope your family's immigration statuses are all in order. Someone— and I have no proof, but I bet you can guess who—called in an anonymous tip to ICE to do a workplace investigation here. They hassled my parents and their employees a lot, even though we're all citizens."

"That's awful. We're safe too, but I'd hate to put my dad and his business partner through that." I glance over at Dad and Mr. Ram, both trying to laugh with their mouths full, careful to avoid spitting out bits of meat. Grandma grimaces.

It's already painfully obvious that we're some of the few folks in Coral Beach with a darker shade of skin not obtained via tanning bed or airbrush. As out of place as I feel sometimes, I don't need some scary van rolling up and fueling that thought in everyone else.

"We need to stop them before they strike again," Ajay says. "Who knows how many restaurants they've done this to."

Across the room, Catalina gives a pointed fake cough. Ajay and I need to get back to our table.

"Good luck," Annie says, noticing Catalina. "I'm sorry you're going through this. But my advice? Cook something else or be prepared to go out of business."

I nod, my mood dark. "Let's go, Ajay."

"I hope they saved enough for us," Ajay mutters, eyeing the diminishing piles of food on the grill.

Annie stands up. "I'll help my grandma bring over more banchan. She's probably excited to see your party enjoying themselves so much. It's been pretty dead in here lately."

"More of those bean sprout things? I love those," Ajay says, already drifting back.

"Thanks, Annie. I'll make sure Dad tips extra well, and I'll five-star review the heck out of this place. Maybe we can get Prime BBBQ back on its feet."

"Maybe." She gives a small, sad smile before turning to the kitchen.

My legs feel heavy as we plod back to our table. This isn't just about the Banana Leaf anymore. It's about Prime BBBQ and the countless other restaurants we haven't unearthed yet. It's about the ones that might fall if Ajay and I aren't able to stop the Darlingtons.

Annie and her grandma bring over two of every kind of banchan—three of those bean sprouts Ajay loves—and I eat up. It'll be fuel for the fire that'll bring the Darlingtons down.

13

THE SUN HAS JUST SET OVER THE EDGE OF the parking lot. My belly threatens to burst and my hair smells like barbecue. Grandma, Dad, Mr. Ram, and Avery mill around the front doors of Prime BBBQ. The eating-contest distraction ended in a draw. Avery inhaled the most plates, but Mr. Ram gobbled up the spiciest kimchi. They awarded Dad the consolation prize of best grillmaster, which he accepted gladly. Annie packed up a complimentary slice of chocolate birthday cake to go for me, because none of us had room for another bite.

Catalina, Ajay, and I stand by Avery's car. Catalina digs for mints in her purse, and Ajay snaps a few artsy photos of the Prime BBBQ storefront. I clutch my takeout cake and the box with the VexHex.

"Thanks for the potion. I hope it does the trick," I say to Catalina.

"You need to have faith," she says, popping a mint. She offers me one. "This magic is in your blood too, you know."

I shake my head. She wasn't there for my failed Brightening Brew in Grandma's kitchen or the times I've attempted, and failed, to make more MettleMix. Of course I have faith: Why else would I continue to even try? It all proves that my magic skills aren't enough, that *I'm* not enough. But I don't want to ruin this otherwise successful birthday dinner by debating it.

Instead, I change the subject. "Thank Avery for me. We couldn't have snuck away for as long as we did without their competitive eating skills."

Catalina slings an arm around my shoulders. Even though we sat right next to each other at dinner, she somehow smells like her almond-scented body lotion, while I reek of chicken. "So what'd you two find out?"

Ajay pockets his phone. "Before they were famous, the Darlingtons ripped off this place's menu for their own restaurant. Like they're doing with the Banana Leaf. And they've apparently got a squad of threatening goons cleaning up after them and keeping everyone quiet too."

Catalina shakes her head. "Do you think you should maybe cool it, then? It's one thing to expose frauds. It's another to expose frauds who have a lot of money and power. I live two hours away, not even counting traffic. I can't swing in to save you."

The way she puts it gives me pause. Dad and Mr. Ram are having a hard enough time scrounging up money for new truck tires—how could they possibly pay for legal bills to fight the Darlingtons?

My grip around Catalina's gift box tightens. With this potion, we may be able to get more of the answers we need. But will it be enough?

"We have to keep going," I say shakily. "We can't let them ruin anyone else's dreams. We'll find a way to blow this up so that there's no way they can touch us." I haven't figured out just how yet, but maybe I'll think better when I'm not stuffed to the brim with banchan.

"I have some ideas on spreading the word," Ajay says. "No way I'm letting them take Ram Uncle's money. Not when he owes me for all this time I've worked at the Banana Leaf already."

I choke. "Wait, you're getting paid?"

Ajay shrugs. "I'll help you renegotiate your job terms once we've saved the Banana Leaf. In the meantime, I've done some research on going viral online."

"You sure you don't want my TikTok army?" Catalina offers.

Behind her, Dad, Mr. Ram, Avery, and Grandma approach. Our short time together is over.

"I'll let you know if I need all forty of your followers," I say, giving her a hug.

"Remember, it's okay if you stop and let Dad handle it. At the end of the day, it's not your mess to clean up. You're just a kid," Catalina whispers. "The Darlingtons sound dangerous. And there are people who won't understand what you're doing. They're going to hate you for this."

The Seashell Squad comes to mind. Elle understands a little, but do I really think all of them will? Especially after how quickly they doubted my suspicions during that mess of a conversation at the Trade Winds?

I pull back from the hug. My mouth sours from remembering yet another risk in saving the Banana Leaf. As hard as I've tried to fit in, I'm going to have to prepare for my new friends to avoid me when this is over.

Am I ready to choose the Banana Leaf and being alone in Coral Beach forever? On our ride home, I fall into a meat-induced nap, uneasy over a question I don't have an answer to.

14

MY PHONE RATTLES WITH A SERIES OF TEXT alerts as I pull my new ultra-soft floral pajamas— Grandma's birthday gift—over my head. More birthday perfection: Carlos and Molly on FaceTime!

"¡Feliz cumpleaños, chica!" Molly screeches.

I grin. You take one Spanish class with someone and suddenly they want to throw their A+ skills at you at every chance.

Carlos bumps Molly out of the way and yells a "Happy birthday!" too. Molly is in her signature pigtails, Carlos looks like he got a fresh head-shave before Kids Baking Camp— he's ultra-paranoid about hair in his baked goods—and they both sport bright blue camp shirts. A pang of sadness hits me at the thought that I'm not there with them.

"I miss you guys. How's camp?"

Carlos shakes his head. "Nuh-uh, we're not talking about camp. We want to hear about the Fab Foodie Brothers!"

Molly shoves her way back on camera. "Carlos almost fainted when he saw you went to the soft opening! Can you imagine if we were there to livestream it? All our YouTube followers would've been so jealous!"

"How was the food?" Carlos cuts in. "The brothers? Tell us everything."

I drag in a breath before launching into how the Fab Foodie Brothers weren't who we thought they were, how I've been trying to find proof that they stole Dad's recipes.

Molly's and Carlos's jaws drop in unison, and that makes me miss them even more.

"No. Way," Carlos says at the end of my explanation.

Molly's eyes narrow. "That's terrible! I wish we could come help you somehow."

My LA friends believe me wholeheartedly. I didn't have to worry that revealing the truth about their culinary idols would turn them against me. Starting over in a new place is so much more complicated than unpacking a suitcase and signing enrollment forms.

"Thanks," I say. "But I don't know how you can help. I'm barely sure my plan is going to work. I'm going to use an albularyo potion."

Carlos's eyes widen. "Like Catalina? That's a great idea. She's so pretty."

"What does that have to do with anything?" I ask.

His light brown cheeks pinken. "Um, nothing. Just saying."

An announcement blares through a loudspeaker on Carlos and Molly's end, and they both frown. "Oh no, we gotta run, Mila," Molly says. "Almost lights-out for us, but we couldn't let the day end without saying hi to the birthday girl! And seriously, let us know if you think of a way we can help. We'll try to sneak more peeks at our phones while we're here."

They hang up, and I stretch back in my desk chair. The clock on my phone says it's almost nine p.m., but my barbecue-filled body suddenly thinks it's midnight. I yawn and open my laptop for my final birthday activity: a call with Mom.

It's been nearly two weeks since I've spoken with her. We used to chat every couple of days, but the connection can be so unreliable in her corner of the Philippines. While I wait for her call, I open the box Catalina gave me.

The VexHex is in a small, amber-colored medicine-dropper bottle—nice of Catalina to think I'll only use one or two drops. At this point, I'll pour the whole bottle into someone's smoothie if it means saving Dad's truck. Next to the bottle is a book. It's black with gold lettering on the front: *Practical Witchcraft of the Philippines.* The creased cover tells me someone's read it over and over.

Something plucks at my heart. Catalina gave me this Filipino witchcraft book that she bought with *her* latte money. I run my fingers over the dog-eared pages. Over the years, she's been on my case about not being in tune enough with my Filipino heritage. Then here, in Coral Beach, I crunch under the pressure to be a cookie-cutter copy of everyone else.

I've always had the feeling that someone's trying to squeeze me into some ill-fitting uniform. They don't listen when I say it doesn't fit, that it's too tight here or the shoes pinch there. It somehow becomes my fault, instead of the uniform that I didn't choose. A stronger, more confident person would stretch and mend the uniform to make it fit, or they'd pick another outfit entirely.

But I'm not sure where I stand. How do I decline that uniform if I've got nothing else to wear? I find myself grinning and bearing it instead. But I wonder if all I'm doing is making myself feel more exposed.

A torn piece of notebook paper flits out of the book when I open it. In my sister's scratchy handwriting is one word: *laban.*

I stare at it before reaching for my laptop and finding a Tagalog-to-English translator.

Fight.

Despite the prickle of shame I feel for not recognizing the word, I smile and smooth out the paper. Catalina believes in what I'm trying to do. And even if she bugs me about not being in touch with my Filipino roots, she's trusting me to learn. Warmth spreads through my chest as I flip through the pages of the book. I feel closer to her and Mom, as if they're reading the ingredients and instructions aloud for me.

A ring blares out of my laptop.

"Happy birthday, Mila!" a blurry Mom sings out from my screen. She waves her hands as if this is the most exciting thing she's done all day, and her enthusiasm is contagious.

"Thanks, Mom! How's everyone there?"

"We're all doing well. Your grandpa and grandma went around the corner to have lunch with some friends, so it's just you and me, my milagro." Mom's smile widens. "My milagro is milagrowing up! Ha!"

I roll my eyes (even though her wordplay *was* actually kind of funny). I catch her up on the birthday dinner eating competition and my surprise call from Molly and Carlos. Mom regales me with stories of reuniting with her childhood best friend, who now owns the premiere halo-halo joint in town. The distance and time difference melt away, and suddenly it's just me and Mom chatting about everything and nothing. But we're missing our lumpy LA couch, the steam from her chamomile tea, and the TV humming in the background.

"Your grandpa's got three more weeks of physical therapy, then a follow-up appointment. And if that's all clear, I'll be buying my ticket home," Mom says.

The mention of her timeline sobers me. That's *after* the opening of Marigold and Myth. By the time she gets back, the damage to the Banana Leaf will already be done.

Her voice cuts through my thoughts. "Anything I can bring you from the Philippines? Your sister asked for some jewelry and a couple books."

I need some hard proof that the Fab Foodie Brothers are scum.

I need to save the food truck because it's the last thing that belongs to us as a family.

I need our whole family together again, because I might not have any friends left by the end of summer.

I gulp away the sadness. "Maybe a beginner's book on folk healing? I can't seem to get any potions right."

Mom's eyebrows furrow. "Mila, you don't need a book. You've got me and your sister. We can teach you."

I'm about to counter that no, I don't actually have her and Catalina, they're both miles and miles away. But that wouldn't help. "I guess. But I tried making Catalina's Brightening Brew and I couldn't get it right. I don't know if I'm even saying the incantations correctly. I don't know Latin or Tagalog or anything. I—I think it's me. I don't think I have it in me to be an albularyo."

"Mila," Mom says softly. "Of course you have magic in you. You have to believe in yourself."

I try not to scrunch my face. "Ugh. That's what Catalina says."

"Your sister is right. When you're creating, focus on the magic and what you want it to do. And don't stress about those incantations. It's not the words—it's the intention. Put your confidence into it, one hundred percent. *Know* it will work."

When she puts it that way, no, I haven't been one hundred percent sure that my potions will work. Maybe it *was* my doubt that affected my magic.

"I'll try, Mom."

"That's my milagro." Her smile warms me like it's made of sunlight.

A quick glance at my laptop tells me it's almost ten o'clock, and I can't help the giant yawn I break into. Mom and I exchange goodbyes, and I close my darkened laptop and stumble over to bed. Mom's words follow me as I drift off to sleep.

Know it will work.

That seems easier said than done.

15

AJAY HOLDS THE AMBER-COLORED BOTTLE up to the light. "So Catalina paid eighty dollars for what looks like my mom's skincare stuff?"

The bottle twinkles in the late-morning sun. It's Wednesday, the first day since my birthday dinner that we can test the VexHex potion. I haven't seen Ajay since the weekend, but we've both been busy trying, and failing, to find more about the Darlingtons' pasts. Dad and Mr. Ram work long days at their other jobs on Monday and Tuesday. Wednesday through Saturday: that's the Banana Leaf's time to shine.

I bite my lip. "But if it works the way I hope it will, then it'll be all her latte money well spent."

He sets the bottle down. We're sitting in camping chairs next to our fold-up aluminum condiment table. Dad and Mr. Ram are in the food truck, getting ready for the lunch rush, which starts in half an hour. Between the two of us, Ajay and I arranged the condiments, wrote up the menu board, and folded a few dozen paper takeout boxes.

Ajay leans back in his chair, the metal frame squeaking as he moves, and my eyes go straight to his jacket pocket. He better not have brought a rat anywhere near our food truck.

"Is that—"

"Relax, Mila. Whirligig isn't on me. He's somewhere safe. I didn't want to risk him falling out of my jacket while you and I were setting up."

I let my shoulders untense.

"Besides, there are more important things to focus on."

"More important than a restaurant-ending rat at our families' food establishment?"

Ajay plants his elbows on the table next to the Mang Tomas bottle. "The grand opening is only three days away. I think your plan is good, but . . ."

I scratch at a dried spot of banana ketchup with my fingernail. "But what?"

"But do you think now is really the time to be relying on some magical oil stuff? Don't get me wrong, that Brightening Brew was amazing. But shouldn't we keep investigating? You know, just in case."

I sigh. "I've been looking for a chance to sneak back into the restaurant, but there's always someone in there. You're right, though—we shouldn't pin all our hopes on this potion. Not without testing it."

Ajay gulps. "How?" He leans away, as if I'm about to pour the whole solution down his mouth.

"Calm down. I'm not going to test it on you."

He sighs with relief. "Then who?"

"All right, crew, here they come!" Dad calls from inside the truck. The glass doors of the white business plaza ahead swing open and worker bees in collared shirts and cardigans file out.

We're one of three food trucks positioned around Coral Cove Plaza during this lunch rush. So far, Wednesdays here have treated us well. As Mr. Ram pointed out, people are out of the lunches they meal-prepped on Sunday, or possibly already sick of them, and are looking for something fresh and fun. That's where the Banana Leaf comes in.

"Psst, here! Ripley, Mila!" Mr. Ram waves Ajay and me over. He pushes a tray loaded with small paper cups at us. "I made some extra roti-wrapped longganisa for samples. Make yourselves useful and get us some business." He smiles wide, but for once I notice the forced optimism behind it. Grandma's mention of the food truck's success—or lack thereof—claws at the back of my mind.

Ajay grabs the tray and stares down at the sliced-up bits of sausage wrapped in bread. "What are these?"

"Our version of burritos," I say. "Dad makes his own Filipino pork sausage, and your uncle rolls out roti atta like a machine."

Ajay pops one in his mouth, and his eyes widen. "Yum. Like a kati roll! Do we have to give these out?"

I snatch the tray from him. "Yes! Don't eat them all. They're for the customers!"

"Can I at least save one for Whirl?"

The blood drains out of my face. "You said he wasn't here."

"Correction, I said he was somewhere safe."

I follow Ajay's nervous gaze to the truck. When I spot a designer shoebox with a few pencil-size air holes poked into it under the sink, I bite back a scream.

Ajay starts to explain but I shush him as people approach. "We are definitely talking about this later!" I force out through my customer-service smile.

A Black woman in a poppy-red dress pauses in front of our menu board. "Adobo with paratha." She squints to read the description. I should've written it out. Ajay's handwriting is atrocious.

"Oh, that sounds delicious," the woman says. "What do you think, Clint? Want to try this Banana Leaf place?"

Clint, an older white man in a short-sleeved shirt and grease-stained blue tie, wrinkles his nose the teensiest bit.

"No. They had that at the Marigold and Myth opening, Whitney. My girlfriend follows those brothers on Instagram."

Ajay takes the tray back from me like he can tell I want to smack Clint over the head with it. How dare Clint stand feet away from me and mention *them*?

Whitney rolls her eyes. "I don't want to do the grilled cheese truck again. Come on, try something new for once."

Ajay strolls over to the customers. "You know, Marigold and Myth isn't even open yet. And I heard they're having some trouble with their decor."

I gather my wits and walk over too. "Delayed a week, at least. Some big problems in that place. In the meantime, why don't you at least try some free samples?" I wave at the roti-wrapped longganisa like I'm a game show host showing off prizes. "They're especially great with a couple drops of our homemade garlic hot sauce."

Whitney nods enthusiastically. "Sure, throw that hot sauce on there!"

I tug Ajay back toward the condiment table and unscrew the tops of the hot sauce and the VexHex. Our backs to Whitney and Clint, I apply drops of both.

"What are you doing?" Ajay whispers.

"They're perfect test subjects! They get along enough to have lunch, but not enough to agree on everything." This is what I'm hoping the staff at Marigold and Myth will be like:

happy to work there, but new or overwhelmed enough to let the VexHex throw them over the edge into complaining. Perhaps about the owners.

"You'd better know what you're doing," Ajay whispers.

Mom's words come back to me. *Know it will work.* I know this will work because Catalina and her albularyo friend made it.

"I do. Now, Catalina says this stuff will only last two, three minutes, max. Then it's out of their systems. So here goes!" I unfold the piece of paper with the incantation and read it aloud. "*Iram et veritas.*" Then I spin back around with the doctored bites.

"Bon appétit!" Ajay says as he hands the samples to Whitney and Clint. They gulp them down.

Now to wait for the potion to kick in. I grab a napkin and pretend to dust the condiment table. Ajay fidgets with the sample tray.

Suddenly, Whitney's back straightens, and her dark brown pupils flash gold. A second later, Clint jerks upright with a loud belch, and the pale gold of the sun swirls in his blue eyes.

"Oh, I love these. We're eating here, Clint. I've decided."

Clint sputters. "*You've* decided? Last I checked, I can make my own decisions, thank you very much."

Whitney turns to him and flicks a braid behind her

shoulder. "Really, now? Because I thought you'd decided to break up with that girlfriend of yours months ago. So how's that going?"

"It's complicated!" Clint bursts out, flailing his arms. "My cat likes her!"

Ajay elbows me lightly in the side. "Is this . . . going well?"

We watch Clint and Whitney snipe at each other—not yelling, but definitely not polite.

"I . . . think so?"

Clint shakes his head at whatever Whitney last said. "I'll just come right out and say it. I don't trust your restaurant recommendations."

Whitney gasps, and her hand goes to her heart. "Excuse me? I have exquisite taste. It's not my fault your taste buds are wimps and you're so prone to diarrhea!"

Next to me, Ajay drops the tray, and his jaw, entirely. With Clint's face as red as Whitney's dress and Whitney naming every failed lunch excursion of theirs, I start picking up our ruined samples.

Sure enough, three minutes later, Whitney and Clint both slouch. Then they look at each other with that "what have I done?" expression that Dad had the last time he accidentally grabbed salt instead of sugar.

"I don't know what came over me, Whit. I'm so, so

sorry," Clint says, the rage red of his face going embarrassment pink. "I totally trust your recommendations. Lunch is on me."

Whitney puts a hand on his shoulder. "I don't know why I told everyone you get diarrhea easily. I just got so . . . *irritated* all of a sudden."

They continue exchanging apologies as Ajay follows me to the trash can across the sidewalk. With a frown, I dump the dust-speckled roti-wrapped longganisa.

Ajay sighs. "Sorry about that. I hate wasting food too."

"Well, it wasn't *totally* a waste."

We turn back to the Banana Leaf, where Clint and Whitney are ordering. Clint even pulls out a five-dollar bill and stuffs it into the tip jar, maybe an apology for making a scene.

My hand goes to my jeans pocket, where the bottle of VexHex is tucked away. "Now we know this stuff works."

And we're going to use it to take down a food empire.

16

So, HOW'D YOU SPEND YOUR SUMMER, MILA? teachers will ask at the start of the school year.

Oh, you know, just hanging out by a dumpster behind my dad's rivals' restaurant. Trying not to step in anything sticky or breathe in the scent of expired dairy. That kind of thing.

And I wonder why I'm having trouble fitting in.

In the alley behind Marigold and Myth, I shift my hold on a cookie basket. The plastic wrap covering it crinkles. Perfectly shaped chocolate chip cookies, alternating with chocolate-chocolate and snickerdoodle, fill the red wicker basket. A gold bow seals the top.

It's all store-bought. Dad may be a whiz with the savory stuff, but he's not a dessert guy. That's why the Mila Special turon lassi sells so well: it's one of our only sweet items.

Ajay and I dotted each cookie with a couple of drops of VexHex before I said the incantation and repackaged everything. Hopefully these cookies are enough to tease out the evidence needed to bring down the Darlingtons, because the bottle's empty.

"You got your phone ready?" I ask Ajay.

"You know it." In one smooth motion, he reaches into his jacket and pulls out a small yellow notepad, a pen, and his phone, which is already livestreaming audio to my laptop.

I connected my laptop to the souvenir shop's free Wi-Fi (I had to buy a soda from Mrs. Gomez for the password). I want to listen in and record everything the annoyed Marigold and Myth staff say to Ajay once the VexHex takes effect.

We decided it'd be best if I didn't show my face in there. Not after their whole crew had to scramble to a commercial break to avoid televising me questioning their bosses. So Ajay, kid of many talents, is going on my behalf.

I eye his bomber jacket and almost gag at the tail swinging out of the front pocket. "Gross! Is that the tail of your . . . pet?" I don't even want to say the word "rat" so close to a restaurant, even if it's a rival's.

Whatever's in his jacket pocket squirms in response to my question, and my stomach somersaults. I resist the urge to pull out some hand sanitizer, because then I'd have to put the cookie basket down, and I don't trust a single surface in this alley.

Ajay tucks the tail back in. "Psh, tassels are *in* right now, Mila. Follow a fashion account or two. And calm down, no one will notice. Whirl and I are a package deal, so you want my help or not?"

I drag in a breath to banish the nausea. "Yes, yes. Sorry. It's probably better I not even ask. Or look at you. Ever."

"Totally agree. Don't worry, I'll keep Whirligig hidden. He's mostly here for emotional support. You heard what Annie from Prime BBBQ said—this is a dangerous game. Now, I'll head toward the front. You ready with those cookies?"

I hand him the basket. Our plan is to pretend the cookies are a thank-you offering in exchange for a few questions for a kids food blog. Once the staff start munching on those cookies, the extreme annoyance will kick in, and—crossing fingers and toes—they'll start bad-mouthing their bosses.

We wish each other good luck and part ways. To disguise myself, I tug on an oversize bucket hat I borrowed from Grandma. She was delighted that I seem to be taking skin protection seriously, because, according to her, I'm getting "too dark" in the summer sun. Catalina would've thrown back something about skin color and colonization, but I instead grumbled a thank-you and ran off to meet Ajay.

I sidle toward the open back door of the restaurant and listen. A moment later, Ajay's voice floats in from the dining area. "Hi, I'm here for *Coral Beach Culinary Kids*, the most popular youth food blog in town. We're doing a feature on Marigold and Myth, and I'd love to ask you some questions."

Plastic crinkles, and I know he's given them the cookie basket. I slink past the restaurant's back door, then sprint down the alley. When I round the corner, I nearly smack into a group of tourists and narrowly dodge an ice cream to the face. By the time I reach the souvenir shop, my breathing's heavy.

"Everything okay, Mila?" Mrs. Gomez asks as I dash in. She pauses her dusting of the postcard stand and her fuchsia-painted lips twist in concern. I've never seen her without lipstick: she and Grandma share that quirk. I wonder if it's a generational thing, to always look a certain way at all times.

I drag in a couple of breaths and smile. "Yeah, I just need to grab my laptop. It should be done charging now. Thanks for letting me use this outlet."

I hobble over to my laptop, hidden behind a kite display, and unplug it. It was already at a hundred percent when I first walked in half an hour ago, but she doesn't need to know that. I purposely pull out the soda I purchased earlier and take a sugary sip.

She nods. "No problem. But you know, electricity has been getting expensive . . ."

I can take a hint. Ajay should be starting his fake interview and I need a reason to stay in the souvenir shop a few minutes longer to capture the full stream of whatever sound his phone is picking up. Fishing out my wallet, I buy an orange soda for him too.

As Mrs. Gomez pushes my purchase across the counter, the chimes above the door ring and Ajay stalks toward me. I don't know what he's doing here. It's too soon. He should be talking to the staff.

"Everything okay?" I whisper. "It's only been a few minutes and I didn't hear any angry chatter over the livestream. Did the VexHex work?"

That's when I notice his face is a shade too pale, and his fingers are fidgeting with something. I nearly drop my soda when I see what it is: my pink Seashell Squad friendship bracelet, the one I haven't seen in days.

"Mila," he says shakily. "They're onto us."

17

DESPITE THE SODA I'VE NEARLY FINISHED, my mouth goes dry. I take the bracelet from him and worry the fraying end where it must've ripped apart. "Who . . . how'd you get this?"

"The fake interview started out okay. One of the designers was telling me about the hand-carved reservations podium. But as we were talking, the Darlingtons' associate hands me this and says, 'I think this belongs to your friend. Stay in your little truck and out of our restaurant.'" Ajay's shoulders slump like telling the tale saps his energy. "I got out of there as fast as I could."

I hadn't given much thought to the lost bracelet after the day the Seashells and I noticed it was gone. I've actually tried not to dwell on that high tea because the memory of clashing with potential friends made me feel so crummy.

Not only did I drop this very limited-edition bracelet in our rival's territory, but one of the Darlingtons' associates found it. And knowing that it's mine? Either they've been watching Ajay and me this whole time, or I made enough of an impression at the soft opening that someone knows the bracelet belongs on my wrist.

My heart splats on the floor when I realize the dangerous impact of all this. "The Fab Foodie Brothers know we were in the back of their restaurant. They know we're out to get them." And as Annie from Prime BBBQ explained, they're not ones to sit back quietly.

Ajay untwists the cap of his soda, and it's then that I realize his hands are otherwise empty.

"The cookie basket . . . ," I begin.

His face falls. "Oh no, their associate took it and said he'd 'take care of it.' You think he'll be able to taste that they're not regular chocolate chip cookies? I got that cardamom hit when you gave me the Brightening Brew."

I gulp. "If he works with the Fab Foodie Brothers, he might know his flavors. We can't risk it: we have to get those cookies back. If any of them realize the cookies taste off, they might know we put something in them. They could report us to the health inspector. Or the police!"

Ajay darts out the door. It takes me a second to grab my laptop and backpack and thank Mrs. Gomez again. He makes it to Marigold and Myth first. But to my surprise, he slows as he peeks in the open front door, then heads for the alley instead. He stops at the dumpster.

Inside, unopened, sits the cookie basket, doctored with an entire bottle of wasted VexHex.

On our way back to the food truck, I try to wipe the stickiness of the soda off my hands. But it clings to me, just like this feeling of dread.

At the dumpster, Ajay made us pour our sodas on the cookies to destroy the evidence. This kid really does know everything.

"Well, if they didn't open the basket, then at least they don't have any idea we tried to poison them, right?" Ajay asks. He tosses our empty soda bottles into the recycling bin as we pass.

I shush him. "We didn't try to poison them! And don't say that so loudly. What are you trying to do, get us arrested?"

"What I'm getting at," Ajay says, ignoring my shush, "is that if they didn't try any of the cookies, they wouldn't know anything was off about them. We'll still get a chance to Vex-Hex them, like you planned."

"Except we used the whole bottle. How am I supposed to get a new batch by Saturday?"

"Can't you brew some? Your sister says this magic is in your blood too."

I shake my head. "I . . . I can't." I run a sticky hand through my hair. "I'm not good at any albularyo stuff. The magic doesn't work for me the way it does for Catalina and my mom."

"But you can try again, can't you? If Catalina can get you the instructions, we can try to re-create it."

"I said I can't!" My hands clench. Memories of every time I tried again—and again and again—bombard me. Catalina and Mom seem so sure that I can do it, that all I have to do is believe. But they don't have the pressure of the entire family business on their shoulders. It's hard to be confident in the face of what'll happen if I fail. "Give it a rest, Ajay! You need to focus on the Banana Leaf. It's like you don't care about the truck at all."

We both stop at the corner, and he eyes me like I've grown two heads. And maybe I have. I haven't been this scared in years. The Darlingtons' success means my family's doom, and my attempts to stop them are falling flat.

"I do care," Ajay says. There's something distant in his voice. "But with the staff onto us and no more magic on our side, I think we should listen to your sister and lay off this whole thing. It's getting too dangerous."

"But you just said—" I can't wrap my mind around his sudden abandonment. "I know it's dangerous, but we need to save the truck!"

"What do you think I've been trying to do all this time?"

I shake my head. He's fighting me when we should be fighting the Darlingtons. "I don't know, but obviously not enough."

I don't recognize how poorly that came out until Ajay goes quiet. The crosswalk light blinks *Walk*, and we cross. Ajay seems to make a point of staying a few steps away from me. "The truck's important to my uncle, but Mila, what else can we do? The city's protecting the Darlingtons, and everyone adores them. We couldn't even get the investigative reporter from channel seven to help us, and it's her job to help the underdog."

A lump grows in my throat. "But you're my friend."

He doesn't respond.

Then I realize what I said. I've spent so much time worried about losing the Seashell Squad that I didn't notice I've had a great friend with me all along. I've been struggling with the idea of being someone I'm not, but Ajay was willing to help me regardless of whether I fit into some Coral Beach cookie cutter.

Now I might've gone and ruined the whole thing.

"Ajay, you heard Tamra. If we get proof, she'll—"

He cuts me off with a long, exasperated sigh. "I don't know how I let you talk me into thinking we could do this. We should've just listened to your dad and Catalina."

"Catalina didn't say we shouldn't try. She said we should wait until things cool off, but she doesn't get it—we don't have that kind of time. Once Marigold and Myth opens, we've already lost. There's no way the Banana Leaf can compete."

"Then maybe it's not that good of a truck," Ajay snaps.

The response knocks the fire out of me, and a cold silence falls between us. We turn a corner and the Banana Leaf comes into view.

A voice booms in our direction. "Carson, you've gotta be kidding me!"

Ahead, Dad and Mr. Kent from the chamber of commerce stand next to the truck. Dad has his hands on his hips and is grimacing like he's bitten into a whole peppercorn. Mr. Ram is peering out the truck window, his lips pursed.

Then I notice the pastel-clad figures nearby: the Darlingtons. I thought they'd left town. The fact that they're still in Coral Beach—and yards away from my family business— can't be good.

Ajay and I exchange a glance before speed walking the rest of the way. Seagulls caw overhead, as if urging us faster.

"I'm sorry." Mr. Kent's apology floats toward us, along with the scent of whatever Mr. Ram's been frying up. "But you know these Friday Concert in the Park spots aren't guaranteed. The lineup each week is randomly selected, and the Banana Leaf wasn't on the list this time."

"But it's Thursday," Mr. Ram says from the truck window. "Our fridges are stuffed with the ingredients we'll need for tomorrow. What are we supposed to do with all that food?"

Mr. Kent wipes a bead of sweat off his temple. "Well, did you get the email confirmation from the chamber on Monday? We send them out every week to those selected for a spot."

Mr. Ram shoots a look at Dad, whose eyes have gone wide.

"I—I'd have to check again. It might be in my spam folder," Dad mumbles, which probably means *no*.

Mr. Kent shrugs. "I'm sure the city can help you find another place to set up tomorrow night, a spot that's just as good."

Dad plucks off his ball cap and drags a hand through his hair, and my shoulders tense. He musses up his hair when I bring home a bad grade or when something on the truck breaks. It's like the smoothness of his hairstyle reflects the smoothness of the path ahead.

"And you've still got a permit to park here for lunch," Mr. Kent continues. "You'll just have to move your truck by four p.m. so the Darlingtons can set up."

I nearly stumble and my hip smacks into a drinking fountain. "The Darlingtons? Of all the restaurants to take our spot, it's them? That can't be random," I tell Ajay.

At the far end of the park, someone's already setting up the concert banner at the amphitheater.

"Our Friday haul is sometimes more than we make at lunches all week," I add. "Mr. Kent's suggestion about finding another place to park isn't a good one."

"The Darlingtons for sure don't need that money. You can see their gold watches from here."

"And they'll be serving *our* food. Will the town even miss us? Will they even care if we're gone, if they're getting the same stuff elsewhere?" The thought breaks my heart.

We come to a stop next to Dad, but he doesn't notice us right away. His attention is on Mr. Kent. "What if we don't move the truck, Carson?"

Before I know it, Chip and Chaz, who have been watching from off to the side, and Ajay and I have all formed a circle around Dad and Mr. Kent.

"You'll move the truck," Chaz says. It comes out like an order, as if he has the right to tell us what to do. But I guess famous folks like Chip and Chaz aren't used to people not giving them what they want. "If you don't, we have ways of *getting* you to move."

At that, Mr. Ram hops down from the back of the truck, tongs in hand like he's ready to swing. "Like what?"

Mr. Kent puts his hands up. "Now, now, no need for threats."

Chip and Chaz laugh as if he's made a joke, and Chip's voice comes out friendlier than his brother's. "Threat? No, no, that wasn't a threat. What my brother was trying to say is that we'd appreciate your cooperation. We got this spot fair and square, just like our good friend Carson here said."

This convenient-to-our-rivals development doesn't feel fair and square at all, and the words burst out of me before I can stop them. "Dad, you can't let them do this!"

All the adults suddenly turn to me like they've just noticed Ajay and I are here.

"I'm handling it, Mila, it's fine," Dad says, anger seeping out of his voice.

Instead of convincing him to fight harder, my presence seems to have had the opposite effect. Dad's back straightens, Chip and Chaz don matching fake smiles, and Mr. Kent whips off his sunglasses and starts cleaning them with the hem of his pink polo shirt. They're all acting guilty, like we caught them in the middle of something raw and real that we weren't supposed to see. Sometimes kids bring out the best behavior in folks, even for only a moment and even if it's obviously faked.

"Yes, this is business. Shouldn't you be off playing some-where? On a slide, or whatever it is children do?" Chaz says to me.

If steam could come out of my ears, it'd burn everyone around me. I swivel to Mr. Kent, the grass crunching under my feet. "This is a onetime thing, right? We can apply for this spot next week?"

The slightest bit of a frown flits across the brothers' faces, and Mr. Kent pauses his sunglasses cleaning. "Of course you can. The chamber will do its drawing and maybe the Banana Leaf will be on the list again. Just make sure to check your email for the confirmation."

Dad's fists relax. "Well, you know I'll reapply for this spot. It'll be in by the end of the day, Carson."

"Ours too, of course," Chip says before turning to Dad with a hand outstretched. "No hard feelings, then? No reason for anyone to be angry?"

Dad shakes Chip's hand because he's Dad the Nice Guy, but stays quiet.

"No reason to be angry," Chaz repeats for his brother. "Because trust me, you wouldn't want to see the Darlingtons angry. No one interferes with our business." Chaz's gaze flits down to me, and a chill runs down my spine.

Was he the one who found my bracelet in their office? He and Chip know what Ajay and I are up to, after my questions at the soft opening and our salon ambush. The bracelet is evidence that we're still snooping around. Is this Concert in the Park stunt their way of getting back at us?

This latest setback scares me more than that surprise health inspection. It seems to confirm that there's a different set of rules for wealthy, famous folks like the Fab Foodie Brothers. Sure, the town claims the Coral Beach food vendor spots are random. But does that hold true when big-name someones show up with loads of money and promises of publicity?

Long after the Fab Foodie Brothers slide into their Gabriel-driven town car, a cloud hangs over the Banana Leaf. Dad and Mr. Ram don't talk about it, or at least not loud enough for me to hear. They focus on prepping for the lunch rush, Mr. Ram's phone blasting a '90s hip-hop playlist. For once, Ajay doesn't ask to sample the food. He doesn't seem interested in speaking to me either.

As I set out the condiment bottles, I can't help but replay every moment of our interaction with the Darlingtons over and over again.

And I don't miss the sinister notes in their words every single time.

18

THE UNEASY FEELING IS STILL WITH ME THE next morning. It makes me want to scream into my rose-printed guest bed pillow.

The Darlingtons were one step ahead with the friendship bracelet and the Concert in the Park spot. I should've known: they've obviously done this before.

I wander into the kitchen, my stomach grumbling. Dad's already there, his earbuds in, likely playing his favorite baseball podcast. I post up at the counter next to him and he plucks out an earbud.

"You want a smoothie?" he asks. "Mango strawberry."

"Sure. But you're going to put kale in it too, aren't you?"

Dad smiles too innocently. "You need the vitamins! You're a growing kid."

Saving all my fight for the Darlingtons, I let Dad ruin a

perfectly good smoothie with kale. I grab us some glasses from the cabinet, and against the whir of the blender, Dad chuckles to whatever the podcasters are joking about in his ears. My chest tightens. I can't bear the thought of the Darlingtons and their goons doing anything to bully him or Mr. Ram.

Annie's options flash before my eyes. Cook something else? No. Those are *our* recipes, and I'm going to prove it . . . somehow.

Go out of business? No way, not when the Banana Leaf was here first.

I have to keep pushing ahead, even if Dad and now Ajay doubt me.

Dad hands me my smoothie before heading outside to help Grandma garden. When we first moved here, she tried to rope me into her gardening hobby (i.e., force me to do the dirty work like haul bags of fertilizer). She eventually got sick of me asking why she'd bother to grow useless plants (sure, hydrangeas are pretty, but why waste energy on something inedible?). So Dad gets to do all the fertilizer hauling, and I water the indoor houseplants now and then.

As I fill up a watering can, I text Catalina about the latest developments, including the wasted VexHex. It usually takes hours for her to respond, so I know it's serious when I get a FaceTime request ten seconds later. I set down the watering can, make sure Dad and Grandma are out of ear-shot, then answer.

"It's all gone?" she shrieks.

I scurry back to the privacy of the guest room. "Every drop. They found my Seashell Squad friendship bracelet in the restaurant, where it shouldn't have been, and knew not to trust us."

Catalina shakes her head. She's outside somewhere, palm trees overhead, and her hair swishes in the wind. "A friendship bracelet? You don't need proof that you're Coral Beach like that. It's like a shackle proving you've conformed. It's—"

"Stop. That's not why I texted." I don't need her digging at me for trying to fit in here. "I have to do something about the Fab Foodie Brothers. So I . . . I need more VexHex, right away."

"I can't. Avery's visiting family this weekend, and I don't have a ride."

Part of me knew it wouldn't be that easy. "Maybe you can get me the recipe from Jeanie, then?"

Catalina raises an eyebrow. "You're ready to try to brew it yourself? That's great, Mila, but, you know, this is a complicated recipe."

Her doubts ring out loud and clear, but my time and options are running out. "Ready? No. But willing to try so I can take down these frauds? Yeah, I guess."

"You have to be more confident than that. I told you, this magic is in your blood. You just need to embrace it."

"You sound like Mom." The bed creaks as I sit on the corner. "I want to embrace the magic, but the magic hasn't embraced me back."

"Yet," Catalina finishes. "It hasn't embraced you back *yet*. I know I sound like Mom, but we wouldn't be trying to develop your skills if we didn't think you were capable. When I was your age, I somehow managed to burn canned soup."

I snort. I remember that. We had to throw out Dad's favorite pot.

"Mila, with your experience in the truck, you're light-years ahead of me in brewing ability. Your heart just needs to catch up. I know you've got the magic in you."

I sit with her words a moment, because hearing that she and Mom believe in me feels like a tight hug.

"I think I'm ready to try again," I say carefully.

A new email alert pops up on my laptop. "Good," Catalina says. "Because as you were thinking, I sent over what Jeanie and I came up with."

I move over to the desk and scan the text. "The instructions look simple enough."

"Yup. Add the ingredients into the hot coconut oil, let it all infuse. I know you've got the skills to do that—you made that huge batch of garlic-herb oil that made your hair stink for days, remember?"

The memory makes me giggle. Afterward, I'd caught Catalina trying to spray me with air freshener as I napped on our lumpy LA couch.

I scroll to the ingredients list. "I can probably get my hands on these herbs at the truck. It calls for pepper, and cayenne pepper's the hottest pepper we have, and we've got coconut oil, ginger . . ." My stomach flops when I read the last ingredient, marked *optional*. "Hair of the intended? I have to get the Fab Foodie Brothers' hair? We didn't do this last time!"

"That's why it's optional. It'll still work if you do the brew and incantation right. But targeting the potion like that will make it pack a stronger punch and last a couple minutes longer."

I tap my fingers on my desk. She's right—it worked on Whitney and Clint and I didn't have to steal any of their hair. Still, I don't have a lot of time left. I'll need to pack as much of a punch as I can . . . but getting the Darlingtons' hair? Where am I—

"A Cut Above the Rest!" I blurt.

Catalina raises an eyebrow.

"That's Elle's sister's salon. The Darlingtons got their hair cut there last week. I'll see if there's even a little bit left somewhere." This may mean more time around dumpsters. Or maybe Elle stole a lock herself. Crushes drive people to do weird things. "I've gotta go. I've got more texts to send."

"Good luck, Mila. You can brew the VexHex on your own. I know you can. Trust in yourself and your abilities, and the magic will follow."

I offer her a thankful smile for the pep talk even as my stomach turns. To be completely honest, I don't know if my skills are enough—if *I* am enough—to pull this off. But after the mess I've made of drawing unwanted attention to the Banana Leaf, I need to do everything I can to save it.

After Catalina hangs up, I text Elle.

Me: Weird question, but you don't have any of the FFBs' hair around, do you?

Elle: Nope, it's in the trash, with everyone else's. Why?

I gulp and take a chance: I type up a text on the bare basics of my albularyo potion plans. She might scoff at the idea of magic or even out me to the Seashells, but I need those hair samples for the VexHex.

I actually sigh with relief when I read her response.

Elle: WHAT? That's so cool! How much do you need?

I don't know if the other Seashells would be as open as Elle is—she's been on my side, more or less, throughout this whole crusade—but I'm glad I've at least got her help.

Dad knocks on my door. "Mila, ready to go? We've got to leave in ten."

We're setting up the truck a little earlier today, to get in more Friday lunch business before we give up the spot to the Darlingtons for the night. The reminder renews that bitterness in my mouth. I head back to the kitchen to reclaim my mango-strawberry smoothie and finish watering Grandma's houseplants.

The Darlingtons' hair could give my brew of VexHex a higher chance of success. I gulp and text Elle more details. A weight lifts off my shoulders when she says she'll try to bag up a sample for me and drop it by the truck later.

I'm going to make her the most delicious, venti-size Mila Special ever.

Once I make my rounds with the watering can, I grab my messenger bag. My sister's other potions clink faintly inside.

I've got a business and a family to protect. But can I do it myself?

19

WHEN MR. RAM AND AJAY ARRIVE, MR. RAM trudges over to the truck like his shoes are made of cement. He smiles at me and says hi, but his face collapses back into a frown when he enters the truck. Then he closes the door, which he only ever does when he and Dad are going to argue about something.

I was going to tell Ajay about trying to brew the potion myself, but Mr. Ram's behavior worries me too much. "What's that about?" I ask.

Ajay is in shorts and that bomber jacket again. Something squirms around his left side, and I shudder even imagining his pet rat within a mile of our truck. I don't mention it, though, because Ajay's eyebrows are pinched in a way that tells me he's not up for joking.

"Ram Uncle says that it's your dad's fault we lost the

Concert in the Park spot. He was supposed to have taken care of the application and double-checked the confirmation."

"That's not true." But to be honest, I didn't know it was Dad's responsibility. I figured Mr. Ram took care of all the business stuff because Dad is, well, Dad. More interested in papayas than paperwork, in sisig than signatures. And with Mom not around to help, it doesn't surprise me that Dad would let this chip fall.

Ajay shrugs, like he doesn't even want to bother arguing. "Well, they're still out of the Friday-night income. Ram Uncle told my mom the truck's needed too many repairs lately and some bank folks keep calling. It'll probably be only a matter of time before it closes."

Even Mr. Ram is losing faith in the Banana Leaf? The disappointment settles on me like that icky skin on cold gravy. How am I supposed to save the business if the business doesn't think it can be saved?

Before I can ask Ajay more, he pops in his earbuds and wanders toward a nearby gazebo. That rat-shaped something shifts around inside his jacket as he sits with his back against a post. I guess he's made his decision, too. The Banana Leaf and I aren't a priority. Considering the short amount of time we've spent together, it stings more than it should.

A tinny bell chimes behind me, and I swivel to see Karina and Elle slowing their bikes to a stop. I smile to hide my surprise at Karina joining Elle. It's just supposed to be me and Elle exchanging lassi for locks. Karina doesn't even eat our food.

"Is it true?" Karina asks. "The Fab Foodie Brothers are showcasing their food early at Concert in the Park?"

Elle must see my smile slip because she immediately follows up with "We're just curious. We'll obviously be getting our snacks from the Banana Leaf."

So Elle hasn't told the other Seashells about me and the Fab Foodie Brothers. That makes sense. Why risk stirring up trouble within her tight circle of friends? She does have a plastic bag peeking out of her backpack, though, which must be the hair sample.

I kick at the ground. "The Banana Leaf won't even be here. We lost our spot."

Karina's and Elle's faces both dip into genuine frowns.

"Oh no, I'm so sorry," Elle says. "Is that a permanent thing?"

I shake my head. But even though it's not permanent, it *feels* permanent. As if one missed Friday, especially one where the Darlingtons will scoop up all our hard-earned business, could mean the end for us.

"That's good. We can try Marigold and Myth's pop-up this week, then head right back to yours next week," Karina says.

This is where I should be brave and tell my friends what I think about their idols. But seeing Karina's excitement and Elle's apologetic look, like she knows we've lost? My courage flits by before I can grab it.

"Let me make you that turon special, Elle," I say with a sigh.

"That sounds great," she says. "Hey Karina, can you, um, check the ballet schedule again? I could've sworn we had a class today."

Karina whips out her phone. "Oh no! I hope I didn't get the dates wrong again!"

Elle angles to slip the bag to me, away from Karina's phone-focused gaze. "These are the sweepings from that morning, but I couldn't separate out the Darlingtons'. You think this will work for your potion?" she whispers.

I stash the sample in my messenger bag. "It'll have to. Thanks."

I step into the truck. Between the Fab Foodie Brothers' hair—mixed in with whoever else's is in this sample—and access to the truck's ingredients, I now have everything I need to brew the VexHex. Well, besides magic, skill, and "trust in myself," as Catalina put it. But those aren't things I can buy or borrow.

When I return a few minutes later with Elle's turon special, their conversation has moved on to shows they've been marathoning, where they're going to bike to next, and the cute lifeguard at the Trade Winds' resort pool.

Elle mentions something about ordering a birthday present for Lane but doesn't give any more details. I smile through a pinch of sadness. I guess I'm still not invited to Lane's birthday party, or else Lane would've talked to me or sent something on the group text.

I didn't think it was possible to be standing this close to friends and feel so very alone.

20

TOMORROW IS THE GRAND OPENING OF
Marigold and Myth: quite possibly the worst day of
my and Dad's lives. I should've known Grandma wouldn't
be supportive. The slam of the dish in the sink confirms it.

She shuts off the faucet and faces Dad and me as we're
chomping burritos at the dinner table. Grandma made her
own dinner and finished eating before us.

"I told you that this food truck was a bad idea, Edgar,"
she says. She snatches up the rose-print kitchen towel as if
she can wipe off her bad mood with it. "If your father was
alive, he would've never let you throw away your schooling
like this."

Dad lowers his burrito and rests his elbows on the polished wooden table. "Ma, I'm not throwing anything away.
It's not like someone yanks back my degree just because I go

part-time to explore something else. And 'let me'? Come on, I'm an adult. I can make my own decisions. You know how much I put into this truck."

The money, the late nights, the time and energy he could've spent with Mom and me instead, perhaps even visited Catalina at school. All of it floats in the air unsaid, like the scent of carne asada.

"And look where it's gotten you. In debt. Living with me. You can't even afford a caretaker for your father-in-law, so your wife had to go." She aims her gaze at me. "Don't you miss your mother, Mila?"

I swallow my bite of burrito. "Yeah, but—"

"See, Edgar? See what you're doing to your family?"

"That's not what I meant," I cut in. Grandma's in a mean mood. Dad needs to know I'm on his side. "I miss Mom, but I don't blame Dad for—"

"It's all right, Mila," Dad says, his brow furrowed. "I know what you meant."

Grandma stares at us banding together over our burritos. Then she shakes her head. "I can't help you, son. You and Mila can stay here, but I'm sorry, my money is locked up in my retirement accounts."

I didn't realize Dad had asked her for money. Our problems must be worse than I thought if he's requesting Grandma's help. I also didn't know that Mom went to the

Philippines because of money. I knew she wanted to be there to help after Grandpa Ben's surgery, but I thought it was for emotional support.

On our drive up to Coral Beach from LA months ago, I was awakened by the sound of my parents whispering. Naturally nosy, I kept pretending to sleep. I remember them talking about housing costs. Mom's voice took on a wary tone as she spoke about staying at Grandma's house instead of an apartment right away, and Dad had slipped a hand off the steering wheel to hold hers. I didn't fully understand it then, even though I had had my suspicions about what was worrying her. It's what everything seems to be about: money.

"I want to help," I cut in.

Grandma wags a finger at me. "No. Coral Beach is our home. Neither of you can be causing any trouble."

Something about her blaming *me* for causing trouble feels like a slap. "I didn't cause anything. It's the Darlingtons who stole our recipes!"

"Mila . . ." A warning note sounds in Dad's voice.

"They like us here," Grandma continues. "We have friends, jobs. I own this house. You were doing well in school. Do you really want to jeopardize that?"

I don't have a response for her. No, I don't want to jeopardize everything. But that might be what it takes to make sure the Darlingtons don't get away with stealing.

Grandma wants us to be model members of the community. To her, this means me fitting in with the Seashell Squad and their well-connected parents. It means Dad excelling in business (preferably full-time, using his expensive engineering degree, but I'm sure she'd be happy if he was at least making enough money to move out).

But that doesn't mean standing by while someone harms us, does it?

At my lack of an answer, Grandma tilts up her chin. "That's what I thought. I'm going to change for my Zumba class."

Once Grandma's bedroom door clicks shut, Dad turns to me. "It'll be fine. Don't you worry about anything. Or do anything." The worry about the health inspector and the Concert in the Park slot swirls in his eyes. "Your grandma is harsh, but she's right."

I offer a weak smile in return. There's no use trying to convince Dad the Nice Guy to fight back. I wonder how much of what he said is a pep talk for himself. My heart squeezes at the thought that Mom or Catalina would've known just what to say to Grandma. It's hard holding up this roof over Dad and myself when two pillars are missing.

"Did you, um, want one of Catalina's potions? Maybe her Brightening Brew or MettleMix will help?"

Dad chuckles. "That's all right, Mila. You keep them.

I don't think they'll work on me right now, but thanks for trying."

Then he reaches for the remote control and turns on the TV. Tamra Wells of Channel 7 News, yet another person who couldn't (or wouldn't) help us, speaks about a city hall meeting. Dad changes the channel to a baseball game.

I stare at him, confused. Of course Catalina's potions would work on him. He used to take Mom's now and then, and Catalina's are the same. Then it hits me. These potions don't create something out of nothing: they amplify what may already be there. The potions won't amplify happiness or bravery if Dad doesn't have any.

We finish our burritos in silence.

I thought I had to choose between fitting in with the Seashell Squad and fitting in with my family.

But with Ajay angry at me and both Mr. Ram and Dad officially out of steam, it's looking like there isn't a place for me with anyone, anywhere.

21

SATURDAY MORNING IS FOGGY AND GRAY. Dad has me up early to prep for Banana Leaf lunch. Normally, I'd grumble, but Marigold and Myth opens tonight. It's only a matter of time before these early Saturday wake-ups for the food truck are over.

I collected the VexHex ingredients yesterday but didn't get a chance to try brewing it. Dad insisted on family time making dessert for Grandma, so I played sous chef (I *did* get to use a blowtorch, so it wasn't all bad). I think it was his attempt to smooth over their mini fight at dinner.

As I brush my teeth, I scroll through the group texts on my phone. Karina shared a TikTok tutorial on how to apply cat-eye eyeliner, and everyone responded with their attempts at following the instructions. Lane poked herself in the eye twice before giving up, and Claire had more of a raccoon-eye look.

I read every single one—I like hearing what everyone's up to—but haven't been sharing what I've been doing. With Mom and Catalina away, I don't even have access to eyeliner. No way I'm going to go rooting through Grandma's makeup stash, not when we're shakily on good terms again.

Today, the Banana Leaf's lunch spot is a small park by the beach, with a few concrete benches facing the water. Ajay's on his phone at the far bench, where he plopped right after finishing the setup tasks Mr. Ram assigned him. With Dad and Mr. Ram easily serving the handful of customers on this slow afternoon, I keep busy with cleanup. Coral Beach's park service has a cleaning crew, but I try to pick up any bit of trash quickly so the seagulls don't gather and annoy potential customers. Already I see a few of them circling overhead, waiting for scraps.

I'm crushing down the cans in the recycling bag and eavesdropping on customers when familiar voices drift past. It's Whitney and Clint, the business park employees on whom Ajay and I tested out Catalina's VexHex last week. They're eating bland corn dogs and undersalted french fries from Corn You Dig It, parked a few cars down.

"The Marigold and Myth grand opening tonight is going

to be fantastic," Clint says. He's in a white T-shirt and cargo shorts for his day off. "I can't wait to see what they've got." He has a smudge of ketchup on his chin. Good.

Whitney lowers her red sunglasses and raises an eyebrow. "I thought you didn't like that fusion food?" They both glance toward the Banana Leaf, and I make a point to angle away so they don't see my face. There aren't any other kids helping at the food trucks, though, so here's hoping they just assume I'm a tiny janitor.

Clint shrugs. "Oh, like the Banana place? It wasn't bad."

Not bad? I resist the urge to chuck one of the empty cans at his head. Too bad Whirligig isn't an attack rat. Or is he? Maybe Ajay's pet has some super-useful talent the same way Ajay is a walking almanac and social media wizard.

Whitney rolls her eyes. "You're seriously the pickiest eater I know. You need to broaden your horizons, dude."

"Broaden my horizons? I put Dijon mustard on my corn dog this time!"

Whitney shakes her head at clueless Clint. "I'm just saying, it's good to try something different. That's why they have all those condiments at Corn You Dig It—the garlic aioli, the spicy pizza sauce, three kinds of mustard—so you can mix it up, try something new, and still end up with something great. Strip all of that away and you've just got a boring old corn dog."

"But I like boring old corn dogs."

Whitney and I both snort at that, and I hope she doesn't realize I'm eavesdropping.

"Anyway, I *am* broadening my horizons. I can't wait to see what the Fab Foodie Brothers do!" Clint says. "It's gotta be ten times better, right? They've got their own TV show. And they're not serving stuff out of the back of a van."

"It's a truck, not a van," I mumble to myself. They don't hear me.

I stomp back toward the truck. The Darlingtons are already taking our business and they're not even officially open yet.

Would it be better, though, to let them win? If we lost the truck and I didn't have to spend all my time and energy making or selling food, then I could be like everyone else. I wouldn't be the girl with the food truck, the one with the "not bad" food that reminds folks my family is different. I'd be one of the Seashells, biking aimlessly around town and burning at the beach all summer.

The second the thought floats through my head, I realize that's not what I want at all. I don't like being the odd one out, of course, but what's the point of being included if I have to betray who I am? Granted, I don't one hundred percent know who that is yet. Catalina's way more knowledgeable about our Filipino heritage than I am, and there are big differences between me and my friends. I always get hassled by Grandma about even thinking of sleeping over at someone's house, for example. She doesn't think it's proper because sleepovers aren't really a thing in our family.

But maybe these differences aren't the huge obstacles to fitting in that I think they are.

It's a hard truth to swallow: the idea that after how hard I've fought, we still might lose our truck. That doesn't mean I have to lose my family and friends too, though, does it? They may like me for me, food truck or not. But the first step in confirming that is to try to make up with the one person who's trusted me all this time. And his rat.

A wind sweeps through the park, as if some unseen force agrees with me. It catches a half-empty fry cup that bounced out of the trash can. The french fries spill out, and the seagulls screech in triumph. Then the paper cup sails to the bench where Ajay's sitting, hunched over his phone.

I know what I have to do. It's like the universe is pointing the way.

I jog to the Banana Leaf. "Dad, got any extra veggie lumpia?"

Without missing a beat, he hands me a paper basket. "Any chili sauce with that? Or Ram's coconut chutney?"

I shake my head. I've got enough inner spiciness today. I peer down at the basket. "This is a lot. Why do we always serve this much in one order?" We could probably scrape up more profit if we served smaller portions for the same price.

Dad shrugs. "Our food is for sharing."

A wistful smile crosses my face. He never cooks in small batches because he's used to feeding a group. He got his start in his home kitchen with my grandfather, a cook in the US Navy. None of the men in our family have been good at creating individual portions.

I stare at the family-size lumpia basket. I guess it's been a while since I've been around people I trusted enough to share something as personal as my family's food.

"I take back what I said. This is the perfect amount. Thanks, Dad."

I chomp one down for strength on the way to Ajay.

"Here," I say, jutting a lumpia at him. "For Whirl. Whirligig. Mister Whirligig?" I don't know how formal to be.

Ajay lifts his eyes from his phone and stares at the lumpia before taking it. "What . . . what is this?"

"An apology. I didn't mean what I said. You've done a ton, and I was frustrated and took that out on you." I lower my eyes, mostly so he can't see the tears starting to form in them. "I just need the Banana Leaf to work out so badly, you know? It means everything to my family, to me. You don't have to help me anymore. I just wanted to say I'm sorry. And sorry for being a jerk about your pet rat."

Ajay's mouth stays pursed as I blurt out my long-winded apology. Then he unzips his jacket slightly and holds the lumpia close to his chest. "What do you say, Whirl? Do we forgive her?"

I force myself not to make a vomit face. I said I was sorry about being a jerk about the rat, and I have to mean it. People have all sorts of gross rodent pets. That doesn't mean Whirligig's going to wreck the truck. In fact, the worst pet we've seen at the Banana Leaf was a fluffy white Maltese who pooped right where people pick up their orders. Whirl has been downright delightful compared to that.

Whiskers peek out of Ajay's jacket, then a tiny pink nose and furry black snout. Then little paws swipe the lumpia from Ajay's fingertips and the whole thing disappears back into the jacket.

"Was . . . was that a yes?" I ask.

Ajay finally smiles, and it's like someone lifts a fifty-pound sack of flour off my shoulders. "Yeah, we forgive you. And honestly, I've been meaning to apologize to you too."

"To me? Why?"

He slouches. "I was a bit of a jerk to you too about your . . . interesting . . . wardrobe. With Dad being all 'I don't want to babysit you during my trip,' I've been trying to shed my kiddie image by mixing up my clothes. It's actually been kind of fun to reinvent myself, but I shouldn't have forced that on you. I was mean about it, and that's not really who I am or want to be. So you be you, Mila, food prints and all."

And against everything I thought I knew about rats understanding human-speak, Whirl seems to squeak in agreement.

Ajay's standoffishness when we first reunited the night of the soft opening makes more sense now. He was trying so hard to show off this certain image that it made him do things that weren't *him*. It sounds like both of us need to find our own paths and define, for ourselves, what these labels mean.

Bits of Whitney and Carl's corn dog conversation come back to me. Maybe the things that make me different actually broaden my horizons. Maybe it doesn't matter whether I'm Coral Beach enough or Filipino enough. All our stories are different, even if we come from the same place or go to the same schools or share the same ancestors. So why, all this time, have I been struggling to strip away the parts that make me special? Why would I ever want to be a boring old corn dog?

I'm Mila Pascual, daughter of Eddie and Eva, of Coral Beach and Los Angeles, of islands across the Pacific and asphalt and food trucks.

I didn't even need MettleMix to bring me to this realization. I can't change who I am, especially if I'm still figuring out all those details, and I shouldn't have to.

Yes, I want to feel like I belong, but it's not my responsibility to mold myself into what people think I should be. It's up to other people—my family, my friends, this whole town—to see *me*.

And if they refuse to? I gulp. I'll frost that cake when I get to it, I guess. But Ajay is proof that there are people out there who like me for me: food prints and all.

Whirligig, bits of lumpia wrapper dotting his furry mouth and pink paws, also seems to like me. That helps too, I guess.

"Thanks, Ajay," I say, offering him another lumpia. "But wait, what would've happened if Whirl didn't take the lumpia?"

Ajay's face goes dark. "I would've had to kill you." When I blanch, he laughs. "Just kidding. Of course he was going to take it. What you said about helping you—"

"You don't have to," I repeat. "I took your advice and asked Catalina for the VexHex recipe. But the apology was the main thing."

"Oh. So I guess you don't want to see who Ram Uncle caught on camera in a social media post three months ago?"

He unlocks his phone before dangling it in front of me.

There's Dad's dark brown arm, handing someone their order. A line of a dozen people extends from the truck. A cluster of folks wait nearby, sipping from plastic cups of turon lassi. I don't know who I'm looking for—the white-haired interior decorator from Marigold and Myth? The dragon-tattooed waiter? Gabriel the associate and bouncer?—but I gasp when my eyes lock onto a familiar silhouette.

Wide, dark sunglasses cover half the person's face. A boring black baseball cap conceals the usually perfect hair. But hours of watching the Fab Foodie Brothers' shows and specials means I know everyone on the show, front and back.

"It wasn't a staff person," I say. "It was one of the Darlingtons themselves!"

I take a moment to rejoice in the fact that I, Mila Pascual, am one hundred percent right about everything. This picture proves that one of the Darlingtons ate at the Banana Leaf months ago, even though they pretended not to know about us. This must be how they stole our recipes. Chip Darlington studied at the top culinary schools in Europe. He's the kind of person who can take a bite of a cookie and tell you, almost to the ingredient, what's in it.

It's not uncommon for someone to order a bunch of dishes and take them back to the office. Dad and Mr. Ram, especially during a busy lunch hour, wouldn't have thought twice about a sunglassed, ball-capped stranger hauling away one or two of every dish.

"You said we should send this to Tamra Wells, right?" Ajay says. "She wanted hard evidence to convince her producers to run a story."

I shake my head. "I think she'll need more. Having a picture of a Darlington at our food truck is one thing. But proving that they reverse-engineered our recipes and used them to build up their restaurant is a whole other monster."

We both peer back at the truck, at Mr. Ram punching orders into the iPad and Dad handing paper baskets to customers. Mr. Ram swings the iPad around so the customer can sign off on their credit card payment.

"Wait. We enter all our orders into the iPad," I say. "If we cross-reference the time of that photo you found, maybe we can figure out what the Darlingtons ordered. And if those match the recipes they're serving or the ones on the whiteboard in their office . . . oh shoot . . ." I trail off, frustrated that I wasn't able to get clean photographic evidence.

I kick at the ground. Ahead, the spilled french fries have drawn a feathery mob. Seagulls swoop down, trying to grab a beakful of potato.

"The Marigold and Myth doors open at six, and all those Fab Foodie Brothers fans are going to make that place a success as soon as the main course is served," Ajay says. "If we're going to stop them, we have to do it now."

He's right. I haven't tried brewing the VexHex, though, and who's to say it'll actually work? And even if I manage to pull that off, how will I get the Marigold and Myth folks to take it? I need ideas, and the help of one or two good friends wouldn't hurt, either.

A few swallows hop around the perimeter of the french fry fiasco. They attempt to dance between the larger seagulls to swipe a fry, but barely get close. The pushy seagulls easily fence them out.

Then a crow alights in the middle of the swarm. Its piercing caw actually sends a couple of seagulls hopping back. While it has their attention, it grabs a fry and flies off.

"That's what we have to do," I whisper.

Ajay, who's been eyeing the birds too, laughs. "What, dump a truckload of fries on the Darlingtons?"

I shake my head, even though the thought of the Fab Foodie Brothers batting away seagulls is rather entertaining.

"I've been a sparrow this whole time, Ajay. We can't take down the Fab Foodie Brothers quietly, on the edges. We're going to have to stand up and yell it out for all the world to hear. We have to be the crow. And I think I know exactly how to do it, if you're still up for helping."

Ajay pockets his phone. "You know it."

Whirligig pipes in with an enthusiastic-sounding squeak. For once, my stomach doesn't threaten to upend itself at the reminder of this rodent.

I rise. "Comb your hair, put on your best shirt, and throw a bow tie on Whirl. We're going to find a way into the grand opening of Marigold and Myth."

22

"STAY STILL!" ELLE SAYS, HOLDING TWO bobby pins between her teeth. She sticks one into the long, wavy black wig half pinned to my head.

I try to remain motionless while stirring the mixture in the metal pot in front of me. The smell of the coconut oil, herbs, and spices fills the kitchen of Elle's family's bungalow. It's the perfect—and only—place to work on our plan, our disguises, and brewing the VexHex in secret. The VexHex actually smells delicious. A shame I'm about to spike a handful of hair into it.

My phone chimes with a new message, and I smile at Molly's latest text.

Good luck tonight, Mila. You got this!

And UGH Carlos insisted I send his awful joke too. How do you say "good luck" to a chef? Break an egg!

She and Carlos convinced their counselors that a great Saturday-night camp activity would be viewing the Marigold and Myth grand opening. While everyone's eyes are glued to the TV, my friends will be secretly cheering me on and ready to livestream their reactions to my Darlingtons takedown. They're even going to post that photo Ajay found of the Darlingtons at the Banana Leaf to get more folks on our side.

I stir the brew according to Catalina's instructions, my whole body buzzing with energy. I appreciate my LA friends' support, but I'm still not entirely sure my plan will work. A new hairstyle and some fake glasses may not be enough to trick laser-eyed Gabriel and the rest of the Fab Foodie Brothers' staff.

As if he hears what I'm thinking, Ajay smiles. "Relax. You look like a completely different person with long hair."

It might be enough to fool strangers, but we'll be dodging Dad and Mr. Ram too. They were invited through the chamber of commerce as a "no hard feelings" gesture for that Friday Concert in the Park mess. But the Darlingtons' people made it clear that the invitation was for them only— apparently, I was too memorable during my last visit.

Dad and Mr. Ram think Ajay and I are going to be hanging out at Grandma's house. And Grandma thinks Ajay and I are spending the evening at A Cut Above the Rest, learning about business or whatever it is adults think is important.

I turn off the stove and sigh. Being spotted by Dad or Mr. Ram could put a quick end to our hastily plotted plan.

I move the pot to the side to let the VexHex cool, careful to keep my head still. "I haven't had my hair this long since . . ." Since Mom was home. She likes my hair long. I realize I haven't actually been around her in what feels like ages, and the thought rattles my already shaken nerves. "Since I was in LA. I've had short hair the whole time I've been in Coral Beach."

Elle steps back, the bobby pins out of her hands and in my hair. "Done."

I reach for my messenger bag to fish out the baggie she brought me.

Ajay scrunches his face. "You're really going to add that?"

"The albularyo's instructions say that adding the hair of the intended will make this stronger. And the Darlingtons' hair is in here somewhere," I say, shaking the baggie. "I'll take any boost I can."

I throw in a hefty pinch of hair shavings and send a silent prayer into the world that this will work. "Now we let this cool before we strain and bottle it up."

To my relief, the color and consistency look just like the original VexHex. But I won't have time to test it.

Elle eyes Ajay, whose curly hair is slicked back in an almost unrecognizable way too. "Let me get one more pass at Ajay with hair spray. Then I'll change so we can leave."

"You sure you want to do this?" I ask. Elle helping to disguise us is one thing. But sneaking Ajay and me into Marigold and Myth crosses the invisible line between with the Seashells and against them.

Elle spritzes Ajay's hair, then sets the hair spray can on the blue-speckled counter. "Of course I do. You can't get into the grand opening without me. And I'm sorry I couldn't sneak away from Silver before. She's needed me at the salon lately, thanks to all the business the Darlingtons' visit brought in. But you know I'm on your side, right? That's what friends do."

I pretend to adjust the wig to shield the blush on my face. She *is* my friend. Now I know that no matter what happens, I'll have her. The thought warms me like hot fudge on a sundae.

Ajay nods into the makeup mirror that Elle propped on the dining table. "Looking good, Ajay," he says. He spins on his heels like he's on the dance floor and points to Elle and me. "Let's roll."

I reach for the strainer and my empty VexHex bottle. I'd thought about bringing the MettleMix too, but there isn't room in my dress pockets. So I mixed a few drops into some guava juice before we came to Elle's. Amping up my courage tonight is key.

My fingers wrap around the handle of the pot. This is it. Time to turn a grand opening into a grand closing.

Crowds gather around the Marigold and Myth storefront. Strobe lights, the kind from Hollywood movie premieres, crisscross the pink sky. Whoever planned the grand opening wanted glitz and glamour. The Darlingtons are all about appearances.

Ajay, Elle, and I stroll along the edge of the crowd, trying to spot a way in.

Elle gasps. "There's Melissa Alvarez from *Quiches and Kisses*!" She grabs my forearm. "And Darcy Scott! His Hollywood restaurant just got a Michelin star!"

The Fab Foodie Brothers' soon-to-be latest triumph has brought out the biggest names on the Cuisine Channel. The chefs wave like movie stars at the cameras—and there are *so many* cameras.

I dip my head so the black wig hides my face. Ahead, I see Gabriel posted at the front doors. He's scanning e-tickets on non-celebrity guests' phones before admitting them.

I grimace. We have e-tickets, but I didn't think Gabriel would be the one checking. He knows my face for sure.

"Change of plans," I say to Elle and Ajay. Originally,

Ajay was supposed to sneak in through the rear entrance while Elle and I used her family's two tickets. "I won't be able to get in through the front door. Which means that you two use the tickets. I'll try the back."

Ajay nods until he realizes what that means. "Wait. So you're responsible for the distraction?"

I grimace. "Yep. Hand it over."

Ajay smirks. "Sure thing. And *it* is a *he*."

He's not wearing his big bomber jacket tonight—Mr. Ram would've spotted him for sure. Instead, he's sporting an expensive-looking blue-and-gold designer fanny pack. He unbuckles it and hands it to me.

As I fasten it around my waist, I feel a squirm through the fabric and shudder. I have to remind myself why I volunteered for this part of the job, because the thought of a rodent within ten feet of me makes me want to faint.

It's for the Banana Leaf, I say to myself. *It's for my family.*

"*Squeak.*"

You can say that again, Whirligig.

I turn and head for the back alley.

23

FROM MY HIDING SPOT BY THE DUMPSTER, I have a full view of the kitchen through a propped-open door. Staff swarm, prepping and plating. There's no way I can get into the dining area without someone seeing me. And that's where my new furry partner-in-crime comes in.

I drag in a breath to steel my nerves, then unzip the fanny pack. With both hands, I lift Whirl out. I try my best to ignore the flip-flopping of my stomach. He's larger than I imagined a rat would be, but then again, I don't spend a lot of time imagining rats.

I hold him at arm's length. "Look, Whirl. I don't like you, you don't like me," I whisper.

"*Squeak.*"

"But it's time for you to shine. If this works, I'm going to make you your own rat-size Mila Special. Got it?"

His whiskers twitch. I'll take that as a yes. I lower him gently to the ground. "Now go find Ajay."

He sniffs the air, and I swear he nods.

As soon as I lift my fingers off him, he sprints toward the back door of Marigold and Myth. I wipe my hands on my dress, then shrink back against the dumpster, as out of sight as I can.

I can't believe I just gave a rat a pep talk. At least I'll have him as a friend when the Seashell Squad disavows me. The thought makes me want to throw up a little.

I wait. A salty breeze from the ocean floods the alley, rustling the palm trees overhead. Music plays from a radio across the street. A car rolls by, the sound of girls' laughter cutting through the bass of nearby volleyball players' music.

"RAAAATT!"

Pots and pans clatter, then comes a stampede of foot-steps. The white-coated kitchen staff stumbles out of the kitchen, half already on their phones.

"Let the Darlingtons know, right away!"

"I'm dialing the pest control company."

"Mom, I'm having the worst day at work."

In the chorus of distracted people, no one hears me padding by. I slip into the empty kitchen, then scan the countertops and stoves. The appetizers have been plated. It's not clear which of the plates will go to the Darlingtons, and

I won't get anywhere near them to dose their servings. That means I have to add a drop of potion to everything. But it'll take me too long to dose a hundred tiny appetizer plates, and the kitchen staff might stroll back in any minute. That's when I catch a familiar whiff of peanut.

They're serving kare-kare, a Filipino oxtail stew with a peanut-based sauce.

I dash over to the stove. Three giant pots, completely full. Curious, I grab a clean spoon and dip it in to sample the sauce. Not bad. In fact, it's downright delicious. Because it's *our* recipe. The savory flavors turn bitter in my mouth.

I take out the VexHex and hold it up to the light. If I pocket this and walk out of the kitchen, I can keep my friends, but I can't keep our truck. If I continue with my plan, I might be able to keep the truck, but who knows if anyone other than Elle will even speak to me at the start of the school year.

Catalina said I have to trust in myself for this magic to work. And I do, because I know who I am: someone who embraces every part of me, even if I'm still trying to figure out what that means. I *never* want to be a boring old corn dog.

I unscrew the bottle, then split the VexHex potion between the three pots. Now for the incantation. I pause, and the panic slips in: What if I pronounce *iram et veritas* wrong? Blowing out a breath, I remember what Mom and

Catalina said: It's not the words. It's the intention.

So I say my intention out loud, with all the confidence I can muster, in the language I know: "May this potion inspire the truth."

My voice doesn't waver. My hand stays steady as I stir the pots.

Then it's time for my last stop, the back office. I sprint over and ready my camera to take a picture of the whiteboard. I flip on the light and take three clear, rapid-fire photos as evidence. With another few taps, I've sent them to Molly and Carlos.

As I head for the double doors to the dining room, I hear the kitchen staff cautiously reentering the kitchen. I bump the doors open with my hip and step through.

The difference in volume almost floors me. A hundred guests are milling about, laughing. A few are swirling glasses of an orange-and-pink cocktail, their faces too red and their voices too loud. Mr. Kent from the Chamber of Commerce takes a selfie with the elephant statue. Dad and Mr. Ram are standing near him, chatting with each other and thankfully *not* looking in my direction.

I spot Elle and Ajay across the room, then gulp when I see who they're with: the rest of the Seashell Squad. I "excuse me" my way through the crowd to join them.

"What's with the wig?" Karina asks after I greet everyone.

I didn't realize they'd all be here. I'm ready to come clean about my plan, but unfortunately now's not the time: the meal could start at any second. So instead, I flip my fake hair dramatically behind one shoulder and give my best movie star smile. "I . . . just wanted to try a new look! Because of all the cameras, you know?"

Karina, whose own blond hair is curled lightly at the tips, nods. She got dressed up too. And so did Lane, whose turquoise eyeshadow makes her hazel eyes shine. Claire has donned a flowy white sundress and that racoon-eye eyeliner, but then again, she's always overdressed. I can't help but notice that pink friendship bracelets circle all their wrists. Mine is still frayed and broken, sitting on the desk in Grandma's guest bedroom.

Lane starts telling us about her own eyeliner fiasco when Ajay nudges my foot.

"Everything in place?" he whispers.

I nod just the slightest. The pocket of his cargo pants rustles on its own. Whirl must've made it to him safely. *What a good rat.*

I can't believe that thought actually entered my mind.

A smattering of applause breaks out in one corner of the room, and I see that the Darlingtons have entered the restaurant, fashionably late to their own grand opening. A film crew tails them, and outside, Tamra Wells checks her teeth in the side mirror of the channel 7 van.

"She—she's here? I didn't think the Channel Seven Sleuths covered events like this," I say. They only do serious meetings and hard-hitting evidence-backed exposés. That's why Tamra wouldn't help us.

But it occurs to me then that just because she didn't help doesn't mean she didn't believe us. She probably feels the pressure to be and act a certain way more than I do. So maybe she wanted to cover this event, just in case.

Ajay winks at me. "Elle and I phoned in an anonymous tip while you were choosing your wig. Well, not that anonymous. Tamra for sure recognized my voice. She doesn't get a lot of calls from twelve-year-olds."

Between Tamra and her cameras, and Molly and Carlos livestreaming, we'll have quite the audience for our success— or failure. Before I can thank Ajay and Elle, an appetizer plate gets dropped into my hands.

"Enjoy!" a faceless waiter says. They've already disappeared in the crowd, leaving appetizer plates in hands in their wake.

Claire takes a bite of the night's first dish, a golden kheema samosa but with a Filipino pork adobo filling. Her full mouth makes an audible *yum* sound as she tosses her head back, her diamond-stud earrings glinting in the lights of the camera crew.

"This is delicious," she says. "So unique."

I freeze the smile on my face. It's not unique. We served it as a special two months ago. But I let this one go.

"I can't wait for the main course," Karina says.

Everyone nods. This time, I join them.

JAY AND I SQUEEZE INTO A BOOTH WITH the Seashell Squad as the Darlingtons announce that dinner's about to be served. The bright magenta of the cloth napkins pops off the gold-lacquered table. The booth seats are a rich, buttery leather. The Marigold and Myth space is truly gorgeous. It's a shame that if I'm successful in driving the Darlingtons out of town, this place will sit empty again.

". . . with granite sourced from a quarry in India and imported here at tremendous expense," Chaz says. He runs his hand along the rosy pink granite of the small bar in the corner. "But it's worth it for the customers of Marigold and Myth."

Impressed oohs and aahs float through the room.

"Check it out while sipping on one of our signature Philippine mango martinis," Chip says. On cue, a waiter appears next to the brothers with a tray holding two drinks. The liquid is orange-tinted on the bottom, red on top, and garnished with a toothpick spearing a mango cube. More oohs and aahs.

Chip and Chaz each grab a glass, then toast each other before taking a sip for the camera.

The more praise they get, the more impatient I am to see the main course. Every second they're on television talking about how great they are, the Banana Leaf is losing customers.

My eyes land on Dad. His mouth is curved into a smile, but his eyes are sad. Like when we waved goodbye to Mom before she left for the airport. He's sitting in the restaurant of two villains who are out to destroy his business and his family, and he's trying to do it with a diplomatic smile.

Yes, he's trying to stay on the good side of the chamber of commerce. Maybe he even believes the Banana Leaf will find a way to stay in business.

But it occurs to me then that maybe Dad is just really good at pretending things are perfect when they aren't. Maybe he *is* scared of the truck failing, or of Mom not being able to come home soon, even if he doesn't show it. Instead he smiles and acts like everything's fine.

Just like I'm smiling, sitting at a booth with girls who might not consider me a good enough friend to choose over their celebrity idols. Whose friendship I earned by covering up all the *different* parts of me, the emotions I feel that don't match theirs.

I'm done pretending things are fine when they're on the verge of breaking. Sometimes, when everything's up in the air, you have to catch what's most important to you. If the rest falls, you just have to hope you can fix it.

The double doors to the kitchen fly open, and waiters stream out with trays of the kare-kare. Folks straighten up in their seats, pull out their phones, whisper to their table-mates.

Chaz grabs a plate and starts describing the kare-kare to the camera. "This oxtail stew was slow-cooked all after-noon. It'll practically fall apart in your mouth. Then we top it off with a garlicky peanut chutney. And to mop up that delicious sauce, we're serving it with buttery lachha paratha, a layered Indian flatbread hand-rolled in-house. This is fusion at its best."

A waiter lays a plate of hot parathas next to the Darling-tons. They tear off pieces and dip them into the sauce. The restaurant-goers mimic their movements and dig into their own dishes.

This is it. My stomach gurgles from the stress, but Lane mistakes it for hunger. "I know, right? This car-ee-car-ee sounds fantastic."

I force a smile as a waiter sets plates in front of us.

Ajay elbows me. "When do you think it'll kick in?"

I think back to when we tested Catalina's VexHex potion at the truck. The results were nearly immediate. But that potion was prepared by my sister and a much more experienced albularyo. "Hopefully any second now. We need to get closer."

I turn to Elle, who's sitting next to me at the edge of the booth, penning me in.

She sets down her napkin. "Good luck," she whispers. Then she rises so Ajay and I can slide out of the booth.

We head for the bar, where the Darlingtons take more bites of their food for the camera.

To my surprise, Elle doesn't sit down. She walks toward the entrance, where Tamra Wells stands with her crew.

I shove down my rising nervousness and regret not bringing more MettleMix. As Ajay and I get closer to the Darlingtons, voices start to grow louder, more agitated. Then a few burps ring out.

"Wait, *everyone's* starting to look upset," Ajay says to me. "What did you do?"

I gulp at the guilt that I dosed *everyone's* food, not just the Darlingtons'. I hadn't thought through the full impact of that. The potion called for the hair of the intended—the Darlingtons—for maximum magical effect. But then I remember what Elle said after the Darlingtons' appointment at A Cut Above the Rest: business was booming. From the looks of it, nearly everyone in this restaurant must have gotten their hair done at Silver's salon.

"Oh no. Everyone's going to go all VexHex on each other. This will get ugly. We have to hurry."

"But the good news is that it worked. You did it!" Ajay says.

Ajay and I pick up our pace, and a man almost collides with me as he backs out his chair in a huff.

"That shirt looks atrocious. The color reminds me of cat throw up," the man says to his tablemate.

"So does your hair," says the other man, a gold flash in his eye.

We weave past them, only to get splashed with mango martini as a woman tosses her drink into her date's face. I catch that same gold glint in her gaze.

"That's it, we're over!" she growls.

"Well, joke's on you, toots," her date says with a grimace. "This drink is delicious, and you wasted it. Just like you wasted your savings on that lemon of a car of yours."

When we finally make it to the Darlingtons, the brothers are still chatting live for the cameras, but their faces are strained.

"That's what I just said, Chip," Chaz says with a forced laugh.

"Yes, but I say it better." He smiles, but there's an angry gold gleam in his eyes and a bead of sweat on his brow.

Now's my chance. The VexHex potion is in their blood, and the whole Cuisine Channel has their eyes on us.

I cough to clear my throat. "Hey, Fab Foodie Brothers, tell us how you got your great ideas," I say loudly. My voice cuts over the sound of the increasingly annoyed crowd.

Chip and Chaz spin to face me, and both their smiles crack. "You!" they screech in unison.

One of their producers, a white woman in an emerald-green tank top, whispers harshly, "Take the question, guys! We're live!"

Their faces perk up so quickly that I almost wonder if I imagined them recognizing me.

Chaz forces another laugh. "Well, we love to chat with our fans, even the youngest ones," he says. "Even if they're brats," he adds under his breath.

"So then tell us! Who was the genius behind these ideas?" Ajay says.

And this is where our plan gets blue-cheese funky. Because I figured that the Fab Foodie Brothers being annoyed with me wouldn't be enough to make them confess. But annoyed with each other? That might tip them over the edge.

I turn to Ajay. "Obviously it was Chip. He's the more talented Darlington."

"Excuse me?" Chaz takes a menacing step toward me before he remembers he's being watched. He forces his stiff muscles loose. "I designed this whole restaurant. All of these ideas are mine."

Chip raises an eyebrow. "Excuse me?" he says in the same tone as his brother. "Not all of the ideas were yours. The food is usually my territory, remember?"

"Right, Chaz, you're not a chef," Ajay cuts in. "You just pick fabrics and stuff."

The whole restaurant starts to chuckle and sneer. This sets a blaze in Chaz's eyes so bright that I almost feel like I'd get burned from standing too close. We might have overdone it.

When Chaz laughs this time, there's nothing amused in it. It's the sound of knives sharpening against each other. "You kids and your jokes. You have no idea what you're talking about."

I glance back at the Seashell Squad, who haven't touched their food yet. Good. At the other end of the room, Dad rips a piece of paratha, and Mr. Ram's already chewing.

It's then that I remember that Dad stopped at Silver's salon last week. His hair might have made it into the VexHex.

After all the times he's tried Mom's and Catalina's potions, he's going to feel this familiar family magic and know I had something to do with it. Then he'll try to stop me.

It's now or never.

"I know exactly what I'm talking about. It was *you*." I point a finger at Chip. "You ate at our truck, the Banana Leaf, back in March, didn't you? I have it on camera!"

Ajay raises his phone, the picture already cued up, and shows it to the film crew. The producer gasps.

"You lied and said you hadn't heard of our truck. But you tried our food, figured out our recipes, and built this place to get rich off our success! And this isn't the first time you've done it either. Anyone here ever heard of Prime BBBQ in San Mariano?"

This is where I expect Chip to confess. Instead, he snorts. A graceless sound, like a horse. "I've never been to this Banana Leaf place in my life. And March? I was out of commission, recovering from an important medical procedure. There's no way I could've . . ."

He trails off, then looks at his brother. "No," he says, his voice shakier. "There's no way. Mort, tell me you didn't. You wouldn't."

That's when Chaz—the easygoing Darlington, always showing off art selections or negotiating silverware prices—explodes.

"It's Chaz!" he shrieks.

I tilt my head. "Wait, your name isn't even Chaz? It's Mort?"

Chip nods. "Morton, like the salt. He changed it so we'd be more matchy, for the show. Just like he makes me cut my hair the same as his and wear contacts instead of glasses."

"For what it's worth, you'd look great in glasses," Ajay pipes in.

Chip casts him a smile. "I know, right? And our last name is really Smorkel. He made us change that too because he thought it wasn't glamorous enough. Ticked off Grammy Smorkel with that one."

My jaw drops. That's why Ajay and I couldn't find anything online about the Darlingtons before 2015. They were Chip and Morton Smorkel! And Morton wanted so much to be embraced by the celebrity chef world that he changed everything about himself *and* pulled his twin brother along for the ride. This VexHex potion is some powerful stuff.

Chaz, or Morton Smorkel, glowers. "Chip, be quiet!"

Chip folds his arms. "No. I'm done being quiet. I can't believe *you* got us into this mess!"

Chaz's hands curl into fists. "Why? Because you're so sure I'm not smart enough? Well, I'm the one who went to that cheap Banana Leaf truck and paid some culinary school students to figure these recipes out. I knew you didn't have the guts to do it again, Chip, not since your last facelift seemed to have opened up your guilty tear ducts."

The air is sucked out of the restaurant with collective gasps. Really? The facelift reveal is the most shocking to everyone?

Energy crackles around me. Not only did my potion work splendidly, but I also got the Darlingtons—at least one of them—to admit they stole our recipes. I *knew* my taste buds weren't lying.

"How could you?" Chip says to his brother. He places a hand on his chest, like his heart is breaking. He truly didn't know. "You swore we wouldn't do this again. I only agreed to this restaurant because you were so proud of coming up with the concept yourself. But now I know—"

Chaz pokes a finger at Chip. "You never had what it takes to succeed. I'm the one who's had to beg, borrow, and steal to get us here. You'd still be Chip Smorkel, fry cook, if not for me!"

All of a sudden, Chip juts a hand out at the camera, covering the lens. "Well, stick a fork in us. We're done, Mort. Show's over, folks!" He storms off.

Chaz looks out at the restaurant full of angry patrons. Including Dad and Mr. Ram, who have had enough VexHex potion to rile them up.

"Get outta here, Fad Fraudie Brothers!" Dad yells. It's the

worst insult I've ever heard him say, and I'm a little proud.

Then Whirl, superhero rat extraordinaire, makes an epic leap out of Ajay's pocket and onto the bar.

"Squeak!"

"RAAAATT!"

All around us, patrons yelp and jump up, knocking over chairs and upending full plates. They scramble out the doors. Some get pulled aside for an interview with Tamra Wells for Channel 7 News.

Next to me, Ajay pockets Whirl and reaches for a celebratory hug. I angle, careful not to smoosh Whirl, as we jump up and down. "You did it, Mila! You drove out the Darlingtons!"

A shadow towers over us. Dad.

"Tell me. Exactly what did Mila do?"

25

THE PRODUCERS USHER US OUT OF THE EMPTY wasteland that was Marigold and Myth. Dad, Mr. Ram, Ajay, and I linger on the sidewalk with a few dozen other patrons who are trying to figure out where to get dinner. Across the street, Tamra Wells continues covering the disaster. She waves and mouths a *good job* when they cut to commercial.

My phone buzzes. Molly and Carlos sent me screenshots of their YouTube comments: pages and pages of folks supporting me and the Banana Leaf. And apparently, Dad's use of "Fad Fraudie Brothers" has caught on online.

A car screeches to a stop in front of our group, and Grandma barrels out. "Mila, you're supposed to be at the salon! Then I see you on TV and—"

"I can explain," I blurt. I draw in a deep breath, then

lay everything out for her and Dad, even the part about getting the VexHex potion from Catalina. I leave out the part about testing it on the Banana Leaf's customers, though. Dad wouldn't love that I used the potions at the truck.

Dad shakes his head. "I told you to let it go. You should have listened to me." Then a smile quirks up his lips. "But more importantly, I should've listened to you. Sorry, Mila."

"The Banana Leaf just means so much to all of us. We couldn't let it go without a fight, right?" I say.

"You were more creative in your fight than I would have been."

Grandma lifts her chin. "Too creative, if you ask me! I wish you could've found a way to do this without making a scene."

Mrs. Gomez wanders by, pats my shoulder, and hands me a cold orange soda from her store. "It's on the house. Good work, Mila." She flashes a smile at my grandmother. "Flora! You must be proud of your girl for exposing those frauds, no?"

"She disobeyed both me and her father. I don't know how I'm going to explain this to everyone at work on Monday," Grandma says. She sounds angry, but her brow has relaxed at her friend complimenting me.

Mrs. Gomez laughs. "Oh, come on, Flora. America loves an underdog story! And what's more underdog than a little girl going up against big business and winning? You'll be a star at the office."

Grandma's face softens then. I don't know if it's because she's finally realizing how much I've done, or if it was simply the idea that underdog stories are an American favorite, but she reaches out and pushes a strand of hair back from my face. "Well, yes, I am proud of her, even if I don't agree with her . . . methods. She did save the day, and against such odds!" She smiles at me. "You really are a milagro."

The blood rushes to my cheeks at the memory of what my parents call me—and the fact that I almost never hear Grandma speak anything other than English. I realize then that even she and I are alike in some ways. When she and Grandpa moved to the US, they spent decades tucking away the parts of themselves that didn't seem to fit in their new American surroundings. I wonder who she would've been if she could've been herself, like I'm learning to be. Maybe we can help each other figure it out.

Mr. Ram drapes his arm over Ajay's shoulders. "You did good, kids. I would've never thought about magicking up their food. I would've been worried about straight-up poisoning them by accident."

Ajay and I share an awkward glance. It's a good thing Catalina and her albularyo boss wrote such detailed instructions.

"What do you think the other business owners are going to do?" Mr. Ram asks Dad. "We drove out the one thing that was supposed to make this place a foodie destination."

Dad runs a hand through his hair. "We'll just have to face the consequences, even if we didn't do anything wrong. I hope we can find a way to keep the truck and the other restaurants alive, together."

I nod. Proving the Darlingtons are frauds is just the end of one problem. There's a lot more to Dad and Mr. Ram running a successful business, but I'm certain that Ajay and I helped smooth the path for them.

Mr. Ram brings out his phone. "Let me text the Corn You Dig It gals and let them know we've got a lot of hungry folks over here."

A tap on my shoulder makes me turn. Elle beams a smile at me. Behind her stand the rest of the Seashell Squad.

Karina clears her throat. "Hi, Mr. Pascual. Can we talk to Mila for a minute?"

Dad nods, and I approach them. But I can't read their faces. Do they hate me?

I start talking first. "So now you know. The not-so-Fab Foodie Brothers stole our recipes, and I've been spending the last two weeks trying to prove it and drive them out of Coral Beach. I know everyone loves them and the business they were supposed to bring to town, so I totally understand if you don't want to be friends with me."

Elle shakes her head. "That's not what this is. I tried my best to explain everything to them, Mila."

Lane tucks a strand of red hair behind her ear. "It stinks to know that our favorite celebrities are actually the worst. But that's nothing compared to the damage they were doing to your dad's business."

Claire nods. "I'm so sorry I thought their food was cool. The Banana Leaf is definitely the coolest."

I scan their words for sarcasm but don't find any. "Wait, so you *don't* hate me for taking down the Darlingtons?"

"Are you kidding? I joined the livestream of these kids in LA, Carlos and Molly Cook It Up. I got over a dozen new followers after chatting with everyone," Lane says. She holds her phone out. "If there's anything the world loves more than celebrities, it's seeing them get taken down. And you, Mila, are the queen of the takeout."

Claire grins. "And can you believe how cool this is going to make us once school starts? We were here when our friend butted heads with the Fab Foodie Brothers . . . and won!"

"I probably won't mention that witchcraft stuff to my parents," Karina adds. Her aunt was the one who thought yoga was too *out-there*. "They'll be pretty upset about that extra business they were counting on. But I think they and all the chamber of commerce folks will come around when I explain that the Darlingtons were threatening my friend."

I can hardly believe my ears. "You'd do that? For me?"

Elle smiles. "You're our friend, I told you."

"But I don't understand. I mean, I don't always feel included with you guys. Like Lane's birthday party on the yacht . . ."

Lane's face crumples. "Sorry, that's my fault. I didn't want to talk about it, but Dad's yacht got repoed."

"Oh no. I'm so sorry." It makes sense that she wouldn't have a yacht birthday party if they didn't have their yacht anymore. "I had no idea."

"Yeah, my parents are going through some financial stuff. It's just hard to admit what's happening, even to friends like you, you know? To risk them seeing you in a different way and not knowing if they'll accept you."

Tears start to prickle my eyes. They still haven't seen the real me, either—the one who's both proudly Filipino and proudly Coral Beach—but that's okay, because I'm working on figuring that out. And now I know there are people like the Seashells who'll understand that friends can change and grow in ways you don't expect. Friendship can change and grow with it.

I offer Lane a hug, and she squeezes me back. And I don't miss that she and the others did, in fact, call me a friend.

Dad twirls the key to the former Marigold and Myth space around his finger. It's been a month since the Fab Foodie Brothers' Filipino Indian fusion restaurant shuttered, right after its disastrous grand opening. Their show is now on indefinite hiatus, and the Darlingtons are under investigation for everything they did to make this and their other restaurants happen at the expense of other local businesses.

According to the gossip sites, the Darlingtons have gotten separate attorneys and aren't even talking to each other. It was confirmed that Chip was not involved in the theft of the Banana Leaf recipes, and he is apparently working with a nonprofit—and a team of publicists—in hopes of swaying the public to his side.

As part of his apology tour, Chip agreed to turn the Marigold and Myth storefront into a pop-up space, an incubator for new restaurants. All the local food trucks will get to use the kitchen for special events, if they get on the schedule. The Banana Leaf gets this space for the next month before Corn You Dig It moves in for a while. We'll continue to share and rotate through the space until the Darlingtons' five-year lease runs out.

"Don't just stand there, help me!" Ajay grunts behind me, holding a box full of dried noodles.

I hold open the door and let him by. Whirl shuffles around in Ajay's fanny pack, but thankfully he's zipped up nice and cozy. Mr. Ram begins to pull the heavy golden curtains open, letting sunlight stream into the empty space.

Elle and Karina trail behind Ajay, boxes of mangoes in their arms. I direct them to the bar, and we locate a blender.

I concentrate on making my Mila Special turon lassi as Elle and Karina help Dad, Mr. Ram, Ajay, and even Grandma unload the rest of the food truck supplies. My friends insisted on helping launch the Banana Leaf pop-up, and Lane and Claire will be here later to livestream Dad and Mr. Ram cooking up pandesal and parathas. We'll even be doing a joint livestream with Molly and Carlos on their YouTube channel.

Catalina and Avery are on their way up to Coral Beach to taste test the food and deliver a new batch of potions. When I asked Catalina for more MettleMix, she had the audacity to laugh.

"Mila, that MettleMix is just water with a dash of hot sauce," she said. "All that courage? That was you. I knew you didn't need magic for that."

Kind of like I said before—siblings: they're helpful even when they're not.

Catalina's also bringing a few used books on Filipino American history she found at the university bookstore— not a requirement, she emphasized, just a suggestion.

Mom already texted to confirm that she and my grandparents will be watching our livestream from the Philippines. We have a family FaceTime after dinner (or breakfast, their time). After I needled Dad about the fact that Ajay was getting paid and not me, Dad put my back earnings into a ticket to the Philippines. The plan is for me to spend some time with Mom and her parents while she packs and wraps up loose ends. More important, we can use the extra baggage allowance that comes with my ticket to bring back ingredients in big balikbayan boxes. Catalina is already making a list of rare items and herbs that she needs me to find while I'm there.

When the truck is empty, Ajay, Elle, and Karina hop onto the barstools, where I have three Mila Specials ready for them. I stick a toothpick with a mango cube on Ajay's glass for you-know-who.

I lift my glass. "To the Banana Leaf."

My friends raise their glasses.

"To Mila Pascual, queen of the takeout!" Elle says.

They clink their glasses to mine, but Ajay pauses before grabbing his straw. "Wait, you didn't put anything in this, did you? No potions?"

I laugh and shake my head, the metal of my taco earrings clinking. "No, no. We're completely out of VexHex. I haven't brewed anything else, and I won't share any potions unless someone asks. Besides, that's Catalina's thing. I'm going to stay out of the albularyo business, at least until I can learn more about it. In the meantime, I'll stick to creating my own nonmagical recipes."

But it's nice to know I *can* create magical recipes, if I want to. I am enough.

We all take a sip of our lassis, and I relish the sweet and slightly tart flavor of the drink I came up with all on my own. I don't miss the twist of Karina's face as she takes a drink from hers, then sets down the glass.

"Oh. Hm. I—I don't really like this," she says. "Not anything against you or your dad's cooking. I'm still so new to the whole Filipino Indian fusion thing."

"That's fine," I say, handing her a can of soda instead. "I know it's different. It's not for everyone, but me? I love it."

To the sound of Dad, Mr. Ram, and Grandma laughing and pots and pans banging, my friends and I share our drinks in this space that has finally begun to feel like home. And it should: home is where the stomach is, after all.

ACKNOWLEDGMENTS

Writing this book didn't take magic, but it did take the support and encouragement of so many wonderful, talented people, and to them I owe a food truck–load of thanks.

To Natalie Lakosil, my agent: thank you for your continued advocacy and expert guidance.

To Amy Cloud: when I say this book didn't take magic, this excludes you. How you help me turn my first drafts into something feels like sheer sorcery!

My thanks to the amazing Clarion team, including Laura Mock, Erika West, Trish McGinley, Robby Imfeld, Emma Meyer, and Sammy Brown. It is such a joy to work with you in bringing my stories out into the world.

To Alane Grace: you did it again with this fantastic cover art!

To my phenomenal writer friends who provided notes,

cheerleading, and the occasional sympathetic ear, including Kalyn Josephson, Alechia Dow, Rae Castor, Alyssa Colman, Koren Enright, Sam Farkas, Jenn Gruenke, Jessica James, Ashley Northrup, and Brittney Arena: this writing journey wouldn't be nearly as fun without you. I'd offer to cook for you in gratitude, but none of us want that (trust me), so in the meantime, please accept my sincerest written thanks.

My thanks also to Kate Heceta for such thoughtful critique; to Asha Allam for your expertise on Indian cuisine and the restaurant world; and to Traci Adair, Jennifer Franz, Brittani Miller, and Rossini Yen for your priceless friendship and doing all the restaurant research for our trips.

To the GW Law/Sparkle Motion folks: I couldn't have written a foodie book without all our fun dining adventures from the DC area to Honolulu to Savannah. Thanks for your friendship, support, and letting me sample your dishes throughout the years.

To my FALSD, NFALA, and Pinay Powerhouse friends: thank you again for your inspiration and support, even as my writing gets less and less legal.

Thank you to Mom, Dad, Reggie, and Lalitha for cooking so much and so well that I just had to write a book about it. And of course, my huge thanks for all the childcare and grace as I tried to juggle everything under the sun, including a newborn, to keep pursuing my dream.

To Ruby and Raja: I hope my stories capture even a fraction of the joy that you two bring me. To Rahul: thank you for being a father extraordinaire, a valuable sounding board, and a relentless promo machine. And to Sandy: thank you for being the best writing paw-tner and paw-blicist I could ask for. I hope they're sneaking you some bites of Filipino-Indian fusion food up in doggie heaven.